SLOWLY AND PAINFULLY, A MAN CLIMBED OUT OF THE HUGE SHIP...

'Is there anything wrong?' Sam shouted up to him. 'Can we help you?' There was no answer, just the hesitant motion of the man's arms and legs.

'I'd better climb up and help him down...'

'He's falling!' Nita screamed.

Ten feet above the ground the spaceman's hands seemed to lose their strength, they could not hold on. He fell, twisting in the air, landing on his side. The two doctors ran to him.

'Easy,' Sam said. 'Free his arm while I roll him onto his back. Careful with it, I think it's fractured.'

'Look at his face! What is that...?'

The man's face was pale and covered with swollen red nodules as large as walnuts, some of them were ruptured and suppurating. The same boils were visible at the open neck of his grey space jumper and on the backs of his hands.

Also by Harry Harrison in Orbit Books:

Deathworld Trilogy:
DEATHWORLD 1
DEATHWORLD 2
DEATHWORLD 3
TWO TALES AND EIGHT TOMORROWS
INVASION: EARTH
PLANET OF NO RETURN
PRIME NUMBER
THE STAINLESS STEEL RAT
THE STAINLESS STEEL RAT WANTS YOU
THE STAINLESS STEEL RAT FOR PRESIDENT
A STAINLESS STEEL RAT IS BORN
LIFEBOAT
PLANET OF THE DAMNED
STAR SMASHERS OF THE GALAXY RANGERS
THE TECHNICOLOR TIME MACHINE
THE BEST OF HARRY HARRISON

HARRY HARRISON

Plague from Space

ORBIT

An Orbit Book

First published in Great Britain by
Victor Gollancz Ltd 1966

First Sphere Books edition published
under the title *The Jupiter Legacy* 1971
This edition 1978
Reprinted 1981, 1984, 1986, 1989, 1991

ISBN 0 7221 4443 1

Printed and bound in Great Britain by
HarperCollins Manufacturing, Glasgow

Orbit Books
A Division of
Macdonald & Co (Publishers) Ltd
165 Great Dover Street
London SE1 4YA

A member of Maxwell Macmillan Publishing Corporation

To
HUBERT PRITCHARD
in memory of the many fine days
since 117

1

Dr. Sam Bertolli hunched forward over the chessboard, frowning so severely that his thick, black eyebrows met and formed a single ridge over his eyes, then slowly reached out to advance his king's pawn one square. He relaxed only when the play screen flashed green—he had made the correct move, the same move Fischer had played in 1973 in Berlin. Then the board buzzed slightly and the opposing bishop slid out on a diagonal and stopped. The computer was playing Fischer's opponent in that historical game, Botvinnik, and the move was an unexpected and subtle one. Sam frowned again and bent over the board.

On the other side of the stainless-steel table Killer turned the page of a magazine: it rustled loudly in the intense silence of the Emergency Room. Outside of the hospital the city rumbled and hummed to itself, surrounding them yet keeping its distance—but always ready to break in. There were twelve million people in Greater New York and at any moment the door could open and one or more of them would be carried in, white with shock or blue with cyanosis. Here on this table —on which they leaned so casually—blood-soaked clothing had been cut away, while the now silent room had echoed with the screams of the living, the moans of the dying.

Sam moved out his queen's knight to halt the developing attack. The screen flashed red—this was not the move that Fischer had played—and at the same instant the gong on the wall burst into clanging life.

Killer was up and out of the door almost before his magazine hit the floor. Sam took the time to slide the chessboard into a drawer so that it wouldn't get stepped on; he knew from experience that he had a second or two before the call slip could be printed. He was right; just as he reached the call-board, the end of the card emerged from a slot in the panel, and as he pulled it free with his right hand he hit the *accepted* button with his left thumb, then hurried outside. The cab door of the ambulance was standing open and Killer had the turbine roaring. Sam jumped in and grabbed the safety handle to brace himself for takeoff: Killer liked to hurl the heavy machine into action with a bank-robber start. The ambulance was shuddering as the turbine revved and only the brakes were holding it back. At the same instant Sam hit the seat Killer released the brake and stood on the throttle—the ambulance leaped forward and the sudden acceleration slammed the door shut. They hurtled down the ramp toward the street entrance.

"Where's this one, Doc?"

Sam squinted at the coded letters. "At the corner of Fifteenth Street and Seventh Avenue. A 7-11, an accident of some kind with only one person involved. Do you think you can keep this hurtling juggernaut going straight for about one hundred feet while I get out the surgical kit?"

"We got three blocks yet before I gotta turn," Killer said imperturbably. "The way I figure it that gives you at least seven full seconds before you gotta grab onto something."

"Thanks," Sam said, swinging through the narrow walkway into the back and unclipping the gray steel box from the wall. He sat down again and braced it between his legs on the floor, watching the buildings and motionless cars whip by. Their emergency call was being broadcast to traffic control, which flashed a warning light on the panel of every car within a four-block radius of the ambulance, ordering them to the curb and bringing all traffic to a standstill. The signal lights turned green in their favor and the warble of their siren kept the street clear of pedestrians. They hurtled through a landscape of frozen vehicles and staring faces where all the eyes turned to follow the rushing white form of the ambulance.

Dr. Sam Bertolli sat stolidly, swaying with the swift motion, his square-jawed face relaxed and quiet. This was Killer's part of the job, getting him to the scene of the emergency, and he considered it foolish to waste his time in speculation as to what he would find there. He would know soon enough. Sam was a big man, with big hands that had black hair curled over the knuckles, intensely dark hair. No matter how often he shaved his cheeks had a blue tone and this, along with the permanent groove that was beginning to form between his eyebrows, gave him more of the look of a policeman or a prizefighter. Yet he was a doctor, and a fine one, in the top five of his graduating class the year before. Within a few

2

weeks, by the end of June, his internship would be finished and he would begin a residency. He had his life under control.

Killer Dominguez appeared to be the direct opposite. A slight man with an oversize head, he was as wiry and nervous as a bantam rooster on an eagle farm. His skinny hands were clamped tightly to the steering wheel, his muscles knotted and tense, while his jaw worked nervously on a wad of gum. A thick pillow propped him up into driving position and his tiny feet seemed to be barely able to reach the pedals—yet he was the best driver on the staff and had started at the hospital only after sixteen years' experience behind the wheel of a hack. The streets of the city were his world, he only felt comfortable when he was hurtling a few tons of steel along them, and as an eighth-generation New Yorker he was attuned perfectly to this life, could imagine no other.

The tires squealed as they turned into Seventh Avenue and headed for the crowd of people on one corner: a blue-coated policeman waved them to the curb.

"An accident, Doctor," he told Sam as he climbed down with the heavy steel box. "He was operating a street elevator, one of those old ones, and somehow got his leg over the edge. Almost tore it off before the elevator stopped. I was just around the corner here, I heard him scream."

Sam shot a quick glance at the policeman as the crowd parted before them. He was young—and a little nervous—but he was holding up. Then the elevator was before them and Sam gave the scene a slow, thorough look before he snapped open the emergency kit.

The elevator had halted a foot below ground level and on its floor lay a heavy, gray-haired man about sixty years old with his left leg buckled underneath him in a pool of dark blood. His right leg was pinched between the metal edge of the elevator and the bottom of the ground level opening. The man's eyes were closed and his skin was waxy white.

"Who knows how to work this elevator?" Sam asked the crowd of staring faces. They were moved aside by a teenage boy who pushed rapidly through from the back.

"Me, Doc, I can work it, nothing to it. Just press the red button for down and the black one for up."

"Do you just know how it works—or have actually worked it?" Sam asked as he pushed his telltale against the inside of the patient's wrist.

"I've worked it, lots of times!" the boy said with injured innocence. "Brought boxes down for—"

3

"That's fine. Take control and when I tell you to, lower the elevator a foot. When I say *up* bring it up to ground level."

The dials of the telltale registered instantly. Body temperature below normal, blood pressure and pulse too low and too slow for a man of this age. Shock and probable loss of a good deal of blood; there was certainly enough of it on the elevator floor. Sam saw that the right pants leg had been cut open and he spread the flaps of cloth wide. The man's leg had been almost completely severed just above the knee and there was a black leather belt around the stump cutting deep into the white flesh. Sam looked up into the worried eyes of the policeman.

"Did you do this?"

"Yes. I told you I was near when it happened. We're not supposed to touch a case except in an extreme emergency. I thought this was one—the way the blood was pumping out he was sure to be dead quick enough no matter what else was wrong with him. I pulled off his belt and put it around his leg, then he passed out."

"You did the correct thing—he can thank you for saving his life. Now get the crowd back and tell my driver to bring the stretcher."

Sam's hands never stopped while he talked, taking the powered tourniquet from the box and pushing the stiffened tongue of metal under the injured leg. As soon as it emerged a touch on the switch restored its flexibility; he wrapped it around the leg and inserted the end into the control box. When the sliding spheres were positioned over the major blood vessels he flicked on the power and it tightened automatically, applying the correct pressure to cut off all flow of blood.

"Take it down," he said, giving the man an intravenous injection of 0.02 mg. of ephinephrine to counteract some of the effects of shock. The elevator shuddered and dropped. The man groaned and rolled his head from side to side. Sam looked at the injured leg: it was very bad. Caught between the two metal edges it had been chopped through and almost severed, the femur was sheared and the lower part of the leg dangled, connected only by some skin and the crushed remains of the rectus and sartorius muscles. He made a quick decision. Slipping a large, razor-sharp scalprum from the kit, he took a firm grip below the bloodstained knee with his free hand and severed the connecting flesh with a single stroke of the blade.

4

With the amputated limb wrapped in sterile sheeting and the injured man pulled away from the edge, he had the elevator brought back to ground level. Killer was waiting with the stretcher and, aided by the policeman, they lifted the wounded man onto it. With a professional flick of the blanket Killer covered him to the chin, then wheeled the stretcher toward the waiting door of the ambulance. They moved smoothly, an experienced team, and while Sam latched the stretcher to the wall Killer closed the door.

"In a hurry, Doc?" he asked as he climbed into the driver's seat.

"As fast as you can without any sharp turns, I'm giving him plasma."

As he spoke Sam pulled the tube down from the overhead container, broke the seal on the sterile needle and slipped it into the antecubital vein in the patient's forearm through the swabbed skin.

"How's he doing, Doc?" Killer asked, accelerating smoothly into the emptied street.

"Good as can be expected." Sam strapped the recording telltale to the flaccid wrist which, in addition to displaying the vital information on its dials, made a continuous recording of everything on a small disk. "But you better get through on the radio so they can set up the operating room."

While Killer made the call Sam turned the ultraviolet spotlight on the injured man's chest to reveal the invisible tattooing there: blood type, blood groups, date of birth and drug allergies. He was copying these onto the form when the overhead speaker scratched to life.

"Perkins here, in emergency surgery, I'm washing up. What do you have?"

"I have an amputation for you, Eddie," Sam said into his lapel microphone. "Right leg severed four inches above the patella. Patient is sixty-three years old, male, blood type O . . ."

"What happened to the leg, Sam? Are you bringing it in for me to sew back on or should I start warming up one from the locker?"

"I have the old one here and it will do fine after a little debridement."

"I read you. Give me the rest of the report and I'll start setting up for him."

There were orderlies waiting on the receiving platform to throw open the door and wheel out the patient.

5

"You'll need this too," Sam said, passing over the sealed bundle with the leg. There was only a single space left on the report form now; he entered the time of arrival here and slipped the filled-out form into the holder on the side of the stretcher as it passed. Only then did he notice the unusual bustle around him.

"Something big, Doc," Killer said, joining him, his nose almost twitching as he sniffed excitement. "I'm going to find out what's going on." He headed quickly toward a group of orderlies who were piling up sealed boxes at the edge of the platform.

Something was definitely going on, that was obvious. At the far end a truck was being loaded with medical supplies, while next to it two interns were climbing into a waiting ambulance.

"Dr. Bertolli?" a woman's voice asked from behind him.

"Yes, I am," he said, turning to face her. She was a tall girl whose eyes were almost on a level with his, greenish-gray eyes with a steady gaze. Her hair was a natural red that bordered on russet, and even the shapeless white lab smock could not conceal the richness of her body. Sam had noticed her before in the hospital—was it in the staff cafeteria?—but had never spoken to her before.

"I'm Nita Mendel from pathology. There seems to be some sort of emergency going and Dr. Gaspard told me I would be going out with you."

She was not wearing a pin, nor did she have a cap on, so Sam was sure she couldn't be a nurse.

"Of course, Doctor, this is our ambulance here. Do you know what's happening?"

"Nita, please. No, I have no idea at all. They just called me out of the lab and sent me down here."

Killer hurried over, feverishly chomping on his wad of gum. "Here we go, Doc. Hello, Dr. Mendel, must be big if they dragged you down from the seventh floor." Killer knew everyone in Bellevue and heard all the gossip. "There is something big brewing but no one knows what. Hop in. The Meatball Express leaves in six seconds."

"Where are we going?" Sam asked, looking at the dozen boxes labeled MEDICAL EMERGENCY KIT that had been shoved in on the floor of the ambulance.

"Kennedy Airport," Killer shouted over the whine of the turbine, making a tire-squealing turn around the corner and diving into the mouth of the Twenty-third Street Tunnel under the East River.

The two doctors rode in the back, sitting opposite each other, and there was no way that he could avoid noticing that her lab coat was very short and, when she was seated, rode well above her knees revealing a most attractive length of tanned leg. Much nicer than the last leg that he had brought under his arm. He would rather look at this kind. The medical profession tended to be stern, sterile and well ordered, so that whenever a bit of visible femininity managed to penetrate he went out of his way to make sure that he appreciated it.

"The airport," she said, ". . . then it must be an accident. I hope it's not one of the Mach-5's—they carry seven hundred passengers . . ."

"We'll find out soon enough, there should be something on the radio." The sunlit mouth of the tunnel was visible ahead and he called through to the cab. "There might be a news broadcast, Killer, tune in WNYC."

As they came out into the open Ravel's *Bolero* swelled from the loudspeaker. Killer tried the other stations, but none of them were carrying a news broadcast so he switched back to the official city station as the one most likely to get the news first. They tore down the deserted expressway with the *Bolero* throbbing around them.

"I've never rode an ambulance before, its quite exciting."

"Weren't you ever on emergency duty while you were interning, Nita?"

"No, I stayed on at Columbia after I had my M.D. because cytology is really my field . . . have you noticed, the road is empty of traffic?"

"It's fully automatic, a radio warning is sent to all cars for miles ahead so that they've pulled over by the time we reach them."

"But—there aren't any cars pulled over, the road is just empty."

"You're right, I should have noticed that myself." He looked out of a side window as they roared by one of the entrance roads. "I've never seen this happen before—there are police blocking that entrance and they're not letting any cars through."

"Look!" Nita said, pointing ahead.

The ambulance rocked as Killer eased it over to an inside lane to pass the convoy, seven bulky Army trucks rumbling after a command car, bouncing and swaying at their top speed.

"I don't like this," Nita said, her eyes wide. "I'm worried. What could be causing it?" She was suddenly very female and very little like a doctor: Sam had to resist the impulse to reach his hand across to hers, to reassure her.

"We'll find out soon enough, anything this big can't be concealed for long . . ." He stopped as the music died in midswell and an announcer's voice came on.

"We are interrupting this program to bring you an important news flash. Two hours ago satellite tracking stations were alerted by the lunar radio telescope that an unknown object had been detected approaching the Earth along the plane of the ecliptic, and this was quickly identified as the 'Pericles,' the ship designed to penetrate to the surface of the planet Jupiter . . ."

"But—it's been years!" Nita gasped.

". . . would not respond to attempts at radio contact. This continued after the 'Pericles' went into orbit around the Earth, making six revolutions in all before breaking orbit with what the space service has called very faulty control of the rockets, and then proceeded to make a landing approach. However, in spite of all radio and visual warnings, the 'Pericles' did not attempt to land at either Sahara or Woomera spaceport but instead made an almost vertical descent on Kennedy Airport in New York. Normal flights were interrupted and there was a certain amount of damage that occurred during landing as well as feared loss of life. Stay tuned for further bulletins . . ."

"How—how bad can it be?" Nita asked.

"It could be pure hell," he said grimly. "There must be two thousand flights a day in and out of the field and it sounds as if they had very little warning. Then it depends where the spacer landed, far out on the runways . . ."

"Or on the buildings!"

"We don't know yet. But I do remember that the 'Pericles' is as big as an apartment house and just about the toughest thing ever constructed by man. It would be hard to hurt the ship but I pity anything it sits down on top of."

"But why—it seems so stupid! Didn't they know any better?"

"You heard the news, they said the ship was badly controlled. It's been out there for over two years, no one ever expected it to come back. There's no telling what shape the

8

survivors are in and I suppose that it's lucky they were able to land at all."

"Mother of God—look at that," Killer said between tight lips, pointing ahead through the windshield.

The expressway rose up here on giant pillars in order to span the complex traffic junction where the Long Island, city and airport traffic met. From the summit of this arching bridge they could see across the width of the airport, over the low, widespread buildings and hangars. A new structure had been added to this scene, a dark bulk that rose high up, five times higher than the control tower, a rounded and scarred mass of metal as wide as a city block. There was a haze of smoke across the scene—then everything vanished as they swooped down from the bridge.

"Could you see where it was?" Nita asked.

"Not clearly—but it was away from the passenger depot, I'm sure of that."

Policemen—and military policemen—waved them on, guiding them through the maze of access roads and into a gate that led directly onto the field itself. A policeman held his hand up for them to stop, then threw the driver's door open.

"You got the medical boxes from Bellevue?"

"Yeah, in back," Killer jerked a thumb over his shoulder.

"They want them, over by the SAS hangar, I'll show you where." The cop pushed in next to Killer and held onto the open door. There was grease on his face and his uniform was wrinkled and dusty. "That's it, where the other ambulance is, you can stop behind it. What a goddamn mess. That blowtorch came straight down, cooked a D-95 taking off, blew another one out of the air, landed right on a fuel truck. It's not sorted out yet. I never seen bodies like this. . ."

The policeman jumped out when they stopped and called to some nearby mechanics to unload the medical boxes. Sam started to help Nita down when a haggard-looking police captain appeared.

"Are you doctors?" he asked.

"Yes," Sam said. "Where do they need us?"

"Look, I think there are enough medics here, there was a charter flight of doctors to a convention that we found, it's the supplies we need most right now. But there was a report from the tower of a company jet last seen on the taxiway when that damned thing set down. I haven't checked on it, there was too much to do here. Could you take a look, it would be around the other side somewhere. All air traffic has been diverted, you can cut across the field."

"Of course, we'll go now, did you hear that, Dominguez?"

"We're rolling, Doc—better hold on," Killer shouted, gunning the heavy ambulance into a leap like a jackrabbit. Sam knew what was coming and caught Nita around the waist before she fell. Killer threw the switch and the rear door closed while they raced ahead. "That thing is really a monster," he said.

The ambulance curved in an arc around the base of the "Pericles" like a bug circling a tree, keeping clear of the churned-up soil and buckled slabs of concrete that were still smoking from the landing. The Jupiter rocket was shaped like a squat artillery shell with the rounded swellings of rocket tubes about its base. It was built of incredibly thick metal, they could tell this by the meter-deep holes that had been gouged in the sides without penetrating, and it was grooved, scarred and pitted like a piece of furnace slag. They could only stare at the great bulk in silence while they swept out and around it.

"There's the plane ahead," Sam shouted, and Killer jammed on the brakes.

They saw at first glance that there was very little they could do, nevertheless they tried. The small jet had been flipped onto its back and crushed, then burned into a twisted and blackened ruin. Sam managed to pry the side door partly open and one look at the charred bodies inside was enough.

"We better get back," he said. "They may need our help." He put his hand under Nita's arm, ostensibly to steady her over the broken ground, but he had seen her face go white.

"I—I don't know if I can be of any help," she said. "I never practiced after I took my degree. I've been in research, in the lab. . ."

"It's just like school—you'll be all right. It hits us all like this the first time, but you'll find your hands automatically doing all the things that you have learned. And I'll bet that you're a good doctor."

"Thank you," she said, some of the color coming back. "For helping. I didn't mean to make a fool of myself."

"You're not a fool, Nita. There's nothing to be ashamed of in not enjoying the sight of sudden death, particularly as drastic as that . . ."

"LOOK!" Killer shouted. "Up there!"

There was a squealing from the side of the ship, about twenty feet above the ground, and bits of metal flaked down. A circle appeared and a portion of the ship ten feet in diameter began to revolve like a giant plug.

"It's the air lock," Sam said. "They're coming out."

2

From the other side of the mountainous ship there came the distant rumble of engines, an occasional shout and the clank of heavy machinery, but the sounds were dwarfed by the bulk of the spacer. Other than this an unnatural quiet hung over the airport, an oppressive silence, undoubtedly the first time in years without the scream of jets or roaring of propellers. A flock of starlings settled onto the nearby, churned-up earth, pecking at the suddenly exposed insect life. Overhead a gull drifted in from the ocean on motionless wings, only its head turning quickly, trying to see if the starlings had discovered anything edible. It dipped a sudden wing tip in alarm and swooped away as metal squealed on metal and the great weight of the outer door of the air lock swung free.

"Unload the surgical and medical kits, Killer," Sam ordered, "then get around to the police and tell them what has happened. Fast!"

The sound of the ambulance died away and the thin whine of an electric motor could be heard inside the ship, growing louder as the massive door, now free of the threads, swung out on its central pivot. As soon as the opening was large enough a jointed metal ladder dropped down, unrolling as it fell, stopping almost at their feet. A man appeared in the opening above them and dangled his legs over the edge, groping for the rungs with his toes, then began a slow and painful descent.

"Is anything wrong?" Sam shouted up to him. "Can we help you?" There was no answer, just the hesitant motion of the man's arms and legs. "I'd better climb up there and help him down . . ."

"He's falling!" Nita screamed.

Ten feet above the ground the spaceman's hands seemed to lose their strength, they could not hold on. He fell, twisting in the air, landing on his side. The two doctors ran to him.

"Easy," Sam said. "Free his arm while I roll him onto his back. Careful with it, I think it's fractured."

"Look at his face! What is that . . . ?"

The man's skin was pale and covered with swollen red nodules as large as walnuts, some of them were ruptured and suppurating. The same boils were visible at the open neck of his gray space-jumper and on the backs of his hands.

"Furunculosis of some kind," Sam said slowly. "Though I've never seen anything quite like it before. You don't think—"

He didn't finish the sentence, but Nita's gasp ended it for him. When he raised his head he found himself looking into her widened eyes and saw there the fear that he knew must be mirrored in his own.

"Topholm's pachyacria," she said so softly he could barely hear it.

"It might be something like that, we can't be sure—but we'll still have to take every precaution." He remembered what had happened then.

The bacteria that had infected Lieutenant Topholm during the stay of the first expedition on Venus had not produced any symptoms until after the return to Earth. There had not been an epidemic, yet a great number of people had died and there was still men whose feet and hands had to be amputated who could attest to the virulency of the disease. Since that time the quarantine of spaceships had become more strict to avoid any recurrence of alien infection.

Sam was galvanized into sudden motion by the sound of approaching engines; he jumped to his feet and ran toward the returning ambulance, which was being followed by two police cars.

"Stop!" he shouted, standing directly in their path with his arms raised. Brakes squealed as they halted and the police started to climb out. "No—don't come any closer. It would be better if you backed off at least fifty yards. A man came out of the ship, and he's sick. He's going into tight quarantine at once and only Dr. Mendel and myself will remain close to him."

"You heard the doctor, get them back," the police captain said hoarsely. The two cars backed up but the ambulance didn't move.

"I can help you, Doc," Killer said casually enough, though his face was drained of blood.

"Thanks, Killer, but Dr. Mendel and I can handle this. No one else is going to get exposed until we find out what is wrong with the man. I want you to get back there with the others, then call the hospital and report exactly what has happened so that they can contact public health. I'm bringing the man in—unless they order otherwise—and if I do we'll need the tight quarantine ward. Then seal off your cab and make sure that your gas closures are screwed down tight. Let me know as soon as you hear anything. Move!"

"You're the doctor—Doctor." He managed a crooked smile and began backing up.

Nita had both medical kits open and was strapping a recording telltale to the spaceman's wrist. "The radius seems to be fractured," she said without looking up when she heard his footsteps approaching. "Respiration shallow, temperature one hundred and five. He's still unconscious."

He kneeled next to her. "You can move away and I'll take over—there's no point in having both of us exposed, Nita."

"Don't be foolish, I'm as exposed by now as I'll ever be. But that doesn't matter—I'm still a physician."

"Thanks." His worried face broke into a smile for a brief second. "I can use your help . . ."

The sick man's eyes were open and he made a muffled gargled noise deep in his throat. Sam gently opened the spaceman's jaw with a tongue depressor and examined the inside of his mouth. "Parrot tongue," he said, looking at the characteristic dry, horny surface produced by severe fever. "And the mucous membranes in the throat seem to be swollen as well." The man's eyes were fixed on his face as the throat contracted with effort. "Don't try to talk, you can't with a throat like that . . ."

"Sam—look at his fingers, he's moving them as if he were writing. He wants to tell us something!"

Sam pushed a heavy marking pen into the man's hand and held the clipboard up so that he could write. The fingers moved clumsily, leaving a shaking mark: he used his left

13

hand and he was probably right-handed—but his right arm was broken. With a tremendous effort he scrawled the twisting lines onto the paper, but collapsed, unconscious again, before he could finish. Sam eased him slowly back to the ground.

"It says SICK," Nita said. "Then, it looks like INCH—no it's IN, then SHIP. *Sick in ship*—is that what he meant to write?"

"Sick in ship . . . sickness in the spaceship. He may have been trying to warn us of infection there—or tell us that there are others in there. I'll have to go see."

Nita started to say something—then stopped and looked down at the telltale. "His condition hasn't changed, but he should be in the hospital."

"We can't move him until we have orders from the public health people, so make him as comfortable as possible. Don't try to set his arm, but do put the supporting brace on it. I'm going to look into the ship. Put on isolation gloves before you touch him any more, that will lessen the hazard of accidental infection from those suppurating boils. I'll do the same thing myself before I climb the ladder."

The gloves, really elbow-length gauntlets, were made of thin but very tough plastic, and they each pulled on a pair while he inserted filter plugs into his nostrils. Sam slung the medical kit over his shoulder by the carrying strap and quickly climbed the hanging ladder. When he clambered through the threaded, circular opening he found himself in a metal, boxlike room as wide as it was high and featureless except for a large door on the far wall flanked by a telephone unit. It was obviously a space lock, and the inner door should lead into the ship. A control panel was set next to it and Sam pressed the button labeled CYCLE OPEN.

Nothing happened; the controls were dead and the inner door was sealed. Sam tried all the buttons, but there was no response. He turned to the telephone and found a list of numbers mounted next to the screen. There was the ping of a bell when he dialed 211 for the control room and the screen came to life.

"Hello, is there anyone there? I'm calling from the air lock."

An empty acceleration couch almost filled the screen, and behind it, out of focus, were banked racks of instruments. There was no answer, nor did he see any movement. Sam dialed the engine room next, with the same negative result. After this he went to the top of the list and dialed every number on it, one by one, hearing his voice echo in compartment after compartment. There was no answer. They were all empty. The sick man must have been alone in the ship.

When Sam started back down the ladder he saw that more cars had arrived, but all of them were keeping their distance. A policeman started forward from one of the cars and at the same time an amplified voice boomed out.

"Dr. Bertolli, your hospital wants to talk to you. The officer is bringing you a portable telephone; would you please pick it up."

Sam waved that he heard and, after setting down the medical kit, went to pick up the phone where it had been left midway between the spaceship and the cars. "How is the patient?" he asked Nita when he returned.

"He seems to be losing ground, pulse weaker, breathing shallower and his temperature is still high. Do you think he should have an antipyretic, or antibiotics—?"

"Let me talk to the hospital first."

An image appeared on the small screen when he switched it on, divided in two for a conference call. On one side was a heavyset, gray-haired man, whom he had never seen before, on the other was the worried face of Dr. McKay, the head of the Department of Tropical Medicine and former head of the team who had developed the treatment of Topholm's pachyacria.

"We've heard about the man from the ship, Dr. Bertolli," McKay said. "This is Professor Chabel from World Health. Could we see the patient, please."

"Of course, Doctor." Sam held the phone so that the pickup was focused on the unconscious spaceman and at the same time gave the readings from the telltale and described what he had found in the ship. He then showed them the message the spaceman had written.

"Are you positive that no one else is in the ship?" Chabel asked.

"I'm not positive, because I couldn't get in. But I called every compartment that had a phone; no one answered my calls nor did I see anyone—alive or dead—in any of these compartments."

"You said that you couldn't operate the space-lock controls."

"The power was off, they seemed to be deactivated."

15

"That's good enough for me," Chabel said, coming to a decision. "The controls worked when the man came out, so he must have turned them off himself. That, along with his warning about sickness in the ship, is enough reason to act. I'm going to quarantine that spaceship at once and have it sealed and sterilized on the outside. It's going to be isolated and no one will go near it until we find out what the disease is."

"Bring him to the hospital," Dr. McKay said. "All the patients in the tight quarantine ward have been transferred to other hospitals."

"Should I administer any treatment first?"

"Yes, our experience has been that normal supportive treatment is recommended. Even if the disease is an alien one it can only affect the patient's body in a limited number of ways. I would suggest antipyrine acetylsalicylate to bring the fever down, and a broad spectrum antibiotic."

"Megacillin?"

"Fine."

"We'll leave in a few minutes."

Nita was already preparing the injections when he hung up. They were done quickly while the ambulance backed toward them, the rear door gaping open. The first vertijets appeared as Sam was rolling out the stretcher. They must have already been on their way during the phone call and were just waiting for the go-ahead signal from World Health. There were two of them that circled the spaceship slowly, then vanished behind its bulk. A bellowing roar broke out and clouds of dense black smoke appeared.

"What's happening?" Nita asked.

"Flamethrowers. They'll cover every inch of the ship with them and the ground around. Every precaution must be taken to see that the infection isn't spread."

When Sam turned to latch the door he saw the starling on the ground nearby, dragging its wing in circles. Human beings weren't the only ones who had suffered when the "Pericles" landed—the bird must have been hit by a piece of flying debris. And there was another bird, injured too, lying on its side with its beak open.

3

Killer outdid himself. He knew that the patient was desperately ill and that the sooner he was in the hospital where all its complex facilities could be marshaled to aid him the better his chances were—but this circumstance was only the trigger. As the ambulance's turbine whined up to speed he saw that the police had opened a lane for him directly to the highway, which had been completely cleared of all traffic. When the speedometer hit one hundred he kicked in the overdrive and kept his foot on the floor, screaming the heavy machine down the center of the concrete roadway. Green and white police copters paced him on both sides and another copter dropped down between them: sunlight glinted from a lens in the side window and he knew that the scene was going out on television to the world, they were watching *him*. He gripped the wheel tighter as they hit the turn at Flushing Meadows, keeping speed and turning sharply so that they broadsided into it, skidding sideways through the arc of road and leaving long streaks of black rubber on the white surface. Television!

In the rear of the ambulance the man from space was dying. The antipyretic was controlling his temperature, but his pulse was fluttering and growing steadily weaker. Sam turned the UV light onto the patient's chest, but the furunculosis made it impossible to read the medical history invisibly tattooed there.

"Isn't there something else we can do?" Nita asked helplessly.

"Not now—we've done all we can until we know more about the mechanism of this disease." He looked at her strained face and twisting fingers: she was not used to the dark presence of approaching death. "Wait, there is something we can do—and you'll do it much better than I could." He pulled over one of the equipment boxes and unlatched the lid. "Your pathology department will want blood and

17

sputum samples, you might even prepare slides from those suppurating boils."

"Of course," she said, straightening up. "I can do it now and save that much time after we get to the hospital." While she spoke she was laying out the equipment with automatic efficiency. Sam made no attempt to help since right now work was the best therapy for her. He leaned back on the bench, swaying with the motion of the hurtling ambulance, the only sounds in the insulated compartment the hoarse breathing of the patient and the sighing of the air filters.

When Nita finished taking her samples he snapped the oxygen tent over the stretcher, sealing it tight and putting a filter over the exhaust outlet.

"This will cut down the chance of contamination, and the increased oxygen tension should ease the load on his heart."

The hydraulic motors hummed briefly and the rear door swung wide onto the empty and silent receiving platform. "I can give you a hand with the stretcher, Doc," Killer said over the intercom.

"There's no need, Killer, Dr. Mendel and I can do it ourselves. I want you to stay in the cab until the decon team is finished with the ambulance. And that's an order."

"I always do what the doctor says—" His voice cut off as the circuit clicked open.

Sam wheeled the stretcher toward the elevator while Nita watched the patient. Out of the corner of his eyes he saw the waiting technicians in sealed plastic suits carrying spray tanks on their backs. One of them lifted his hand briefly and Sam realized that McKay himself was leading the team, the head of the Department of Tropical Medicine decontaminating an ambulance.

"This elevator is on remote," a voice said from a speaker in the wall when they had pushed the stretcher in. The door closed behind them, then opened again on the sixtieth floor. The corridor was also empty and all of the doors were shut and sealed, waiting for the decon men to follow them up. Ahead of them the first of the thick, vault-type doors of the tight quarantine ward swung open, then sealed itself behind them. The inner door opened.

"Onto the bed first, then get those samples through to the lab," Sam said, and recognized a tone of relief in his voice. The man was still his patient, but the physicians in the hospital would soon be monitoring the case and advising him. Guiltily, he realized that his relief came from the sharing of responsibility: If the patient were to die now the blame would not be all his.

While Nita sealed the samples into the delivery capsule for the lab he took the telltale instruments that were waiting on the bedside table and he attached them one by one. The sphygmomanometer and thermometer were combined in a black instrument no larger than a poker chip. He fixed it to the unconscious man's wrist with surgical glue and it began transmitting at once as the internal thermal switch turned on. It was self-powered and its microminiaturized transmitter broadcast to an aerial in the frame of the bed; Sam checked its operation on the inset monitor screen. Bad, very bad. Connecting the electrocardiograph and the electroencephalograph was more exacting, but he did it swiftly, then the pH and serum analyzer. All of the information, besides being displayed on the monitor screen, was appearing on the screen in the consultation room. Sam clasped his hands tightly, unconsciously, waiting for the report.

The call signal pinged and Dr. Gaspard's face swam into focus on the telephone screen.

"No diagnosis yet, Dr. Bertolli," he said, "other than our agreement that the disease appears to be completely unknown. There is one thing, the patient has been identified by the Space Commission as Commander Rand, Second Officer of the 'Pericles.' His medical history will be on your monitor screen in a moment, it's just coming in from their record section."

"Are there any suggestions for treatment?"

"Just supportive as you have been doing—"

He broke off as the alarm sounded from the monitor screen where a pulsing red light now glowed over the ECG reading.

"Fibrillation!" Gaspard said, but Sam had already torn open the cabinet drawer and removed the coronary stimulator. Weakened by disease and strain, Rand's heart was running wild as the muscles contracted in uncontrolled spasms, no longer pumping blood but shuddering like a dying animal.

Once, twice the strong electrical current penetrated the convulsive heart muscles, stopping the uncontrolled tremors. Then, slowly, it began to beat again and Sam turned back to the instrument cabinet. Nita was already there, taking out the cardiac pacemaker.

"You're sure to need this," she said, and he nodded agreement. As he made the incision in Rand's heaving chest to connect the terminals fibrillation began again. This time he made no attempt to restart the weakened heart by shocking it, but raced to make the connections to the pacemaker.

"Power on!" he said, looking at the waxy skin of the unconscious man. Behind him the life-giving machine hummed quietly, sending out the carefully spaced microcurrents that duplicated the nerve signals that were no longer reaching the damaged heart. It began to beat again, timed by the artificial stimulation, and blood once more surged out through Rand's arteries.

This was the beginning of the end; from this point onward the spaceman's life slipped away from him and he never regained consciousness. It was hours before he died—officially died—but it was clear all this time that there could be no hope for recovery. Only a miracle could have saved him and the watching physicians neither expected nor received this. Sam, with Nita assisting, labored with all the machines and drugs available to them, but it was useless. The antibiotics had no effect on whatever organism was causing the disease and it spread through the entire system with frightening speed. From the symptoms many—or indeed all—of the man's organs seemed to be affected and renal failure and necrosis pushed him closer to that invisible border. Sam was not looking at the monitor screen so that he missed the moment and did not know it had arrived until Dr. Gaspard's weary voice caught his attention.

"There is no longer a reading on the EEG, Doctor. Thank you, you and Dr. Mendel have done everything possible. I don't think—it is clear now—that from the very beginning there was really very little that could have been done."

The screen went blank. Sam slowly, one by one, turned off the battery of machines that had by heroic measures been producing a simulation of life, then stared down at the dead man. For long seconds he stood like this before he was aware of what he was doing, aware enough to force himself to think, to take the next steps. The patient was dead. Finis. Now to the living.

"There's nothing more we can do here," he said to Nita, holding her arm and drawing her away from the bed. She would not take her eyes from the dead man's face until he pulled the sheet over it.

"Into the decon chamber, Doctor," he said. "All of your clothes, everything including shoes and underclothing, go into the incineration hopper, then a complete scrub. The directions are on the wall if you haven't done it before."

She walked toward the door, slowly stripping off the gauntlet-length isolation gloves, then stopped.

"No, you've handled him the most—you should go before I . . ."

"I have some things to do first," he said, urging her on. This time she did not protest.

By the time Nita emerged from the decon chamber wearing a sterile surgical gown and cotton scuffs the room had changed. The bed had been stripped and even the mattress removed. There was no sign of the body until Sam pointed to the square stainless-steel door set into the wall.

"Orders—he's in there. It's not an ordinary morgue setup; if needed it can be chilled by liquid nitrogen. This will make dissection more difficult, but that was the decision upstairs. But of course—you work in pathology, you must know all about this. Will you take over please, while I scrub? The last word from the council upstairs was that we were just to stand by here until we had further instructions."

Nita dropped into the chair; without the pressure of responsibility she was suddenly aware of how tired she was. She was still sitting there when Sam came out. He went over to the equipment cabinet, sliding open drawers until he found the recording telltales.

"We should have done this earlier because if we are going to catch . . . anything . . . we'll want to know about it as soon as possible." She fastened one to her wrist as he went into the pharmacy and began rummaging through the shelves. "I'm filling a prescription, Doctor," he called out and held up a bottle of clear fluid. "Do you know what this is?"

"C_2H_5OH."

"Ethyl alcohol, correct, I see we both went to the same school. There are many formulas for the preparation of this universal solvent but considering the patients'—our—need of instant medication I favor the simplest and most effective."

"Subcranial injection?"

"Not quite so drastic."

He had extracted a container of orange juice from the kitchen refrigerator and was mixing it half and half with the alcohol: then he poured two healthy beakerfuls. They smiled and drank and neither of them glanced at the shining door in the wall though it was foremost in their minds. Instead they sat by the window and looked out over the towers of the city: it was dusk and the lights were coming on, while behind the dark spires of the buildings the sky was washed with sweeps of red, verging into purple in the east.

"There's something I should have remembered," Sam said, staring unseeingly at the darkening sky.

"What do you mean? There's nothing more we could have done——"

"No, it has nothing to do with poor Rand, at least not directly. It was something at the ship, just before we left."

"I don't recall anything; we were alone, then the vertijets came just as we left——"

"That's it, something to do with them!" He turned so suddenly his drink sloshed onto the floor but he didn't notice it. "No, not the copters—the birds, don't you remember the birds?"

"I'm sorry . . ."

"They were on the ground near the ship; I saw them just before I closed the ambulance door. Starlings. There were a few of them that appeared to be injured in some way, I remember at the time I thought they had been hurt when the ship landed—but that's not possible. They weren't there when we came, don't you remember that? They settled down after we stopped the ambulance." He was running to the phone while he was still speaking, thumbing it into life.

Professor Chabel was in conference but broke off at once to take Sam's call. He listened silently while Sam told him about the birds and the worried cleft between his eyes deepened.

"No, Dr. Bertolli, I have had no report on these birds. Do you think there is a connection. . . ?"

"I hope not."

"The ship has been cordoned off and is being guarded. I'll have men in isolation suits go in there and see if they can find anything. You'll get the report of whatever they discover. In the meantime—will you hold on for a moment . . ." Professor Chabel turned away from the phone and had a brief conversation with someone out of range of the pickup. When he came back on the screen he was holding a sheaf of photographs in his hands.

"These are from the electron microscope, prints are on the way to you as well. What appears to be the infectious agent has been isolated, a virus, in many ways it resembles *Borreliota variolae.*"

"Smallpox! But the symptoms——"

"We realize that, different in every way. I said it is just a

22

physical resemblance, in reality the virus is unlike anything I have ever seen before. In the light of this I would like to ask you and Dr. Mendel to aid me."

Nita had come up silently behind Sam and was listening in; she answered for both of them.

"Anything we can do we will, of course, Dr. Chabel."

"You will both be in quarantine there for an unlimited time, until we can learn more about the nature of this disease. And you have the body of Commander Rand there . . ."

"Would you like us to perform the postmortem?" Sam asked. "It would lessen the risk of moving the body and exposing others."

"It is really a job for World Health, but in the circumstances . . ."

"We will be very glad to do it, Professor Chabel. There is very little else that we can do in quarantine. Will you want to record?"

"Yes, we will have the pickups on remote, and we will tape the entire process. And we will want specimens of all the tissues for biopsy."

Even with the ultrasonic knives dissection of the frozen body was difficult. And depressing. It was obvious from the very beginning that Rand's life could never have been saved since his body was riddled by the pockets of infection; there were large cysts in every organ. Sam did the gross dissection and Nita prepared slides and cultures for the waiting technicians, sending them out in sealed containers through the evacuated tube system with its automatic sterilization stage.

There was only one interruption, when Professor Chabel reported that the dead birds—an entire flock of starlings and a seagull—had been found near the ship. The bodies were being taken to the World Health laboratories for examination.

It was midnight before they were finished and all of the equipment was sterilized. Nita came out of the decontamination chamber, her still-wet hair up in a towel, to find Sam looking at a photographic print. He held it out to her.

"This just came in from World Health, from their lab. Those dead birds filled with cysts——"

"No!"

"—and this is what the virus looks like. It appears to be identical with the one that killed Rand."

She took it and wearily dropped into the couch under the window. In the thin cotton gown, it barely came to her knees when she tucked her legs up beside her, and with her face scrubbed clean of makeup she was a very attractive woman with very little of the doctor left. "Does it mean. . . ?" she asked fearfully and couldn't finish the sentence.

"We don't know what it means yet." He was very tired and knew she must be feeling even worse. "There are a lot of questions here that are badly in need of answers. Why did the ship stay so long on Jupiter—and why did Commander Rand return alone? How did he contract this disease—and does it have any connection with the birds? There has to be a connection, but I can't see it. If the disease is so virulent—the birds must have died within minutes of contracting it—how is it that, well, we haven't been stricken yet." He was sorry the instant he said this, but the words were out. Nita had her head lowered and her eyes closed and he realized they were filled with silent tears that welled out on her face. Without reasoned thought he took her hand in his, it was human need in the face of oncoming darkness, and she clutched it tightly. She settled back onto the couch and the photograph dropped from her fingers and slid to the floor: he realized suddenly that she was asleep.

There were plenty of blankets and he made no attempt to move her, but he did put a pillow under her head so that she could rest comfortably and covered her with a blanket. He was exhausted, though not sleepy, so he turned off the overhead lights and lay back on one of the beds with another glass of ethyl-orange juice. What was this plague from space? His thoughts chased themselves in circles and he must have dozed off because the next thing he noticed was the sunlight coming in through the window over the empty couch. It was going to be another warm day. He glanced quickly at his telltale—it registered normal.

"Going to sleep forever?" Nita asked from the diet kitchen, where she was making dish-rattling noises. "It's six-thirty already." She brought him a cup of coffee and he saw that she had her hair combed and tied back and had applied a touch of lipstick; she looked as bright as the new day.

"I was going to call the World Health lab, but decided to wait until you woke up," she said, and turned to the phone. He stopped her.

"Not yet. The news can wait until after breakfast—if there is *breakfast* that is . . ."

"A delicious, home-cooked, handmade breakfast of farm sausages and new laid eggs—it's defrosting right now."

24

"Show me where it is!"

There was an unspoken agreement that they would hold the world at bay for just a little while longer, enjoying the breakfast in the early sunlight that poured across the room. Until they touched the phone they were cut off and alone in these sealed rooms high above the city, in a private universe of their own. She poured more coffee and they sipped it slowly, looking out at the clear sky and sharp-edged, reaching towers of New York.

"Are you from here, from the city?" Nita asked. He nodded.

"Born, bred and abided here ever since, except for the nine years in the UN Army."

"Nine years! I thought that you looked, well . . . a little . . ." She broke off, a little unsure of herself, and he laughed.

"I look a little old to be an intern? Well, you're perfectly right."

"I didn't mean to . . ."

"Please, Nita—if I was ever sensitive about the fact that I was ten years older than all my fellow students in medical school I've long since developed a thick hide. Neither am I ashamed of the time I put in the Army; I wanted to make it my career and I was a captain before I finally decided to leave."

"Was there a—particular reason for the decision?"

"One perhaps, but the idea was a long time growing. My best friend then was Tom, our medical officer, and little by little I began to have the feeling that there was more sense to his job than to mine. He never propagandized me but he answered all my stupid questions and let me stand around and watch when he was operating. What finally decided me was what happened in that village in Tibet; we had airdropped in during the night to get between the Indians and the Chinese. I had never seen poverty or disease like that and I wondered why guns were the only thing we could bring them . . ."

The wasplike buzz of the phone cut across his words and he turned quickly to the kitchen extension and turned it on. Dr. McKay's face swam into focus on the screen. His Department of Tropical Medicine must have worked through the night and it was apparent from the dark shadows under his eyes that he had worked along with them. He was brusque.

"How are you both feeling? Have there been symptoms of any kind?"

25

Sam glanced at the dials of his own telltale, then at Nita's. "All readings are normal and there are no symptoms. Have there been other cases——?"

"No, we've had none, I was just concerned since you both had been exposed." He closed his eyes for a moment and rubbed at his knotted forehead. "So far there have been no other cases of what is now unofficially known as Rand's disease, at least not among human beings."

"The birds?"

"Yes, we've had men out with lights all night, and since dawn there have been more reports, a plague of birds, dead birds. World Health has already broadcast a warning that ill or dead birds are not to be touched and that the police should be notified at once."

"Have any other animals been affected?" Nita asked.

"No, nothing else so far, just the birds, for which we are very grateful. And you two, no symptoms at all, that is very hopeful. That is why you must stay in touch with me, let me know at once if there is anything, well, out of the ordinary. Good luck." He hung up.

Nita sipped at her coffee. "It's cooled off—I'll have to heat some more." She slid two sealed containers into the radar oven. "Everything about this disease is strange, it doesn't fit any of the rules."

"Well, should it, Nita? After all it is a disease from space, from another world, and it should be expected to be alien."

"New but not alien. No matter what an organism is it can only affect the body in a limited number of ways. If the disease were really alien it would have no effect on human beings—if it were, say, a fungus that attacked only silicon-based life . . ."

"Or a bacteria that was only viable at twenty below zero."

"Right! The disease Rand returned with is entirely new to us, but its reactions aren't. Fever, nephrosis, furunculosis and pyemia. Admittedly the infection was spread through his entire body, but there are other diseases that attack a number of organs simultaneously, so it is just the combination of these factors that is new."

Sam took the hot container she passed him and filled his cup. "You make it sound hopeful. I had visions of a plague from space sweeping around the world." Then he frowned in sudden memory. "What about the birds—how do you fit them in?"

"We don't know if they do fit in yet. They might have the same disease—or something like it. If they do have a related disease it will be a great aid if anyone else does come down with the virus that killed Rand. We'll be able to manufacture vaccine then, if we can't come up with a foolproof drug cure first. I wish I could see how the work in the labs is coming."

"I do too—but we'd better resign ourselves to staying here awhile. You're the pathologist so you'll have plenty to keep you busy with those tissue samples. But there is very little work here for an ambulance-riding intern. I think I'll get on the phone and call a few friends around the hospital, try and find out what is going on in the world outside."

Nita was busy all the morning in the small but complete laboratory that was an integral part of the isolation ward. She was vaguely aware of Sam's phone conversations and the hissing chunk of the tube capsules arriving. When she finally took a break near noon she found him bent over a map that he had spread out on the table.

"Come look," he said, waving her over. "This is all of Long Island—Kennedy Airport is here—and I have had the World Health people sending me over copies of all their reports on dead birds. I've entered the location on the map for each report and noted the number of birds found on the site as well. Do you see a pattern?"

Nita ran her finger over the tiny, red-inked numbers. "At first glance almost all of them are along the south shore, with a number of dense patches in Cedarhurst, Lawrence and Long Beach."

"Yes, they have been found only on the south shore so far; you can see that here in Reynold's Channel next to Long Beach they recovered over two thousand dead ducks. Now, did you happen to notice which way the air lock on the 'Pericles' was facing when it opened?"

"No, I was all turned around, I can't be sure."

"I wasn't certain either, so I checked with the airport. The open port faces almost exactly east southeast—like this." He took a parallel ruler and laid it across the compass rose, then moved it to intercept the corner of the airport where the grounded spaceship lay. He slashed a red line from the airport across Long Island and into the ocean. When he lifted the ruler Nita gasped.

"It goes right through Long Beach, through the center of most of the numbers. But it just *can't* be like that—unless the wind was blowing that way?"

"Almost no wind yesterday you'll remember, occasional gusts up to two miles an hour at that time, but nondirectional."

"Are you trying to tell me that the virus that infected these birds came out of that port like a *. . . searchlight beam* and just swept across the country infecting everything in the way?"

"I'm not telling you anything, Nita—you seem to be telling me. I've just transcribed the figures furnished by the police. Maybe the virus was spread as you said; we might be wrong in thinking that an alien organism would have to conform to our rules of behavior. So far nothing in this whole affair fits the rules." He paced the floor, unconsciously slamming his fist into the palm of his other hand.

"And while it's going on I'm trapped in here. If Rand's disease only attacks birds they could hold us here for the rest of our lives, under observation, never sure but still waiting for us to get sick . . ." The phone signal cut him off.

It was Chabel from World Health. He had a haunted look and when he spoke his voice was pitched so low that it was barely audible.

"There is a patient on the way up, Dr. Bertolli, please be ready to receive him."

"You mean——"

"Yes. Rand's disease. A policeman. He is one of the men who were assigned to collecting the dead birds."

4

Nita prepared the bed while Sam waited impatiently for the inner door to open. The indicator light blinked off signaling that the outer door was closed, then the hidden motors hummed and air hissed by the seals before him and, as soon as the inner door had opened wide enough, he squeezed through. The policeman on the wheeled stretcher—still in uniform—was sitting up on his elbows.

"I don't know what I'm doing here, Doc, I'm not that sick, a touch of fever, a summer cold, you know, this time of year," he said it calmly, quietly, as though trying to reassure himself. There were red, suffused patches on his face that could be developing boils. Sam took up the record holder. Francis Miles, age thirty-eight, occupation, police officer, all typed in very neatly, but scrawled across the lower half of the page in large letters was RAND'S DISEASE VIRUS: POSITIVE.

"Well, that's what you're here for, Frank, so we can find out," Sam said, putting the records back without changing his expression. "Now lie back so you don't roll off and we'll see about getting you to bed." He pushed the stretcher into the tight quarantine ward and the massive door swung behind them.

Nita was cheerful and fluffed the policeman's pillow, produced a menu for him to study, saying that he looked hungry, and even found a bottle of beer that had been tucked away in the back of the refrigerator. Sam worked swiftly attaching the telltales to the patient's dry, hot skin and it took him almost fifteen minutes to get them all accurately placed and recording to his satisfaction. In that time the patient's fever went up a full degree. The first boils were already beginning to form when he closed the door of the office and dialed Dr. McKay's number, touching in sequence the dimpled numbers of the induction dial.

"We've been monitoring your pickups," McKay said.

"Are there any recommendations for treatment?"

"They are under discussion——"

"But you must have some suggestions?" Sam clenched his fists, keeping his temper under control.

"There is some difference of opinion. Supportive treatment appeared to have been ineffective with the last case, but it has been suggested that in combination with interferon it might be more effective and a supply is on the way to you now. However hyperbaric oxygen therapy has been successful with related . . ."

"Dr. McKay," Sam broke in, "there is no hyperbaric chamber here, so treatment would mean moving the patient again. You must understand—the instruments can't tell you everything—this man is dying before my eyes. I've never seen a disease progress with the speed of this one. Have you?"

McKay shook his head with a weary no and Sam leaned closer to the phone.

"Do I have your permission to begin supportive treatment with interferon and antibiotics to stop any secondary infections? I must do *something!*"

"Yes, of course, Dr. Bertolli, after all he is your patient and I quite agree with your decision. I'll notify the committee of what has been done."

When Sam hung up he found that Nita was standing behind him.

"Did you hear that?" he asked.

"Yes, you did the only thing. They can't possibly understand without seeing the patient. I had to give him some Surital, six cc's, he was getting excited, almost hysterical, is that all right?"

"It has to be correct because anything we do now is dictated by the patient's needs. Let's see if the interferon has come yet."

The capsule was waiting in the receiving basket and Sam quickly prepared the injection while Nita swabbed the patient's arm. He was lying on his back, his eyes were closed and he was breathing heavily through his mouth. His skin was spotted with the angry red swellings of the boils. Sam gave him a large intravenous injection, the blood stream would carry the interferon to every part of the body, then injected one of the furuncles with a smaller dose.

"We can use that for a control," he said, ringing the injection site with an iodine marking. "Interferon applied locally is always more effective. In combination with the antipyretic we may get some positive results."

There was no dramatic improvement after this, though the policeman's temperature did drop two degrees. McKay and his group monitored everything and suggested variations in treatment. The burly policeman was Sam's patient and he resented their attitude, that the man was a sort of giant guinea pig, though he made no protests. The policeman *was* a guinea pig; if he could be cured the treatment would be available for others.

And there were other cases. They were being routed to New York Hospital, where a special sealed ward, far bigger than this experimental one, had been evacuated and staffed with volunteers. It was difficult to learn how many there were, even the official medical reports were reticent with the facts, while the TV and radio bulletins were obviously stopgap morale builders. Sam had his patient to care for or he would have seethed with frustration at being trapped in the ward while a plague might be growing in the city outside.

"What is that for?" he asked when he saw Nita removing a wire basket of pigeons from the tube capsule. He had been aware of her working in the lab during the past hours, though he hadn't talked to her. She brushed a strand of russet hair away from her eyes and pointed to the desk.

"I have been reading reports all day from the laboratories that are working on the Rand virus and there is one experiment that they haven't performed yet, that would be safest to do here in tight quarantine where we have a patient ill with Rand's disease."

"What experiment is that?"

She shuffled through the papers and pulled one out. "Here is the first report from pathology. It has been found impossible to infect human tissue in vitro with infected cells from Commander Rand. They tried this before he died last night. They also found out that they couldn't pass the virus on to any of the lab animals, monkeys, guinea pigs, rabbits . . ."

"Then—if it can't be passed on you and I can leave quarantine! But how could this policeman have been infected?"

"Just a moment and you'll see. The Rand virus can infect birds, it has taken hold on every species they have tried so far. And then, this is the worst part, the diseased cells from the birds can infect human cells, that's how poor Frank caught it."

"Have they tried this on a human volunteer?"

"No, of course not! Just on resected tissue in vitro and HeLa cells."

Sam was pacing back and forth, unable to stand still.

"It's like the life cycle in schistosomiasis—from man to snail to man—but that's a blood fluke, there is no record of a virus propagating this way. Not this one-to-one business with man infecting birds then birds infecting man right back, but no cross infection within the species—wait, can the birds infect one another?"

"Yes, that's been proven."

"Then—of course—there's the next step, that's why you have the birds here. You want to find out if the human virus will reinfect the birds. If it does, then that means that Frank

31

here and Rand both had the same disease. If they did, once we break the chain of infection it can be wiped out."

Nita had the hypodermic ready. She reached into the cage and caught one of the birds deftly so that it could not move. It cooed lightly and blinked its pink eyes when the needle slid under its skin: Nita slipped it into another cage and put it into a sealed compartment.

"There's one thing missing," Sam said. "Will the virus from the sick policeman infect other human cells; perhaps it has been changed even more by passing through the birds?"

"No, I've already checked that. I'm not set up for it here, but I sent samples of biopyoculture from the abscesses down to the sixth floor; they found they didn't infect human tissue."

Sam went to inspect his patient, who was sleeping quietly. There was no change, the spread of the disease seemed to have been checked, at least temporarily, though the fever had not gone down. He went back to the lab and sat down across the desk from Nita, who was making notes on a clipboard.

"The lab is beginning to call them Rand-alpha and Rand-beta," she said. "I suppose that will become the official name."

"What's the distinction?"

"Rand-alpha is what Commander Rand had, a deadly virus that cannot be transmitted to man or to any animals other than birds. Rand-beta is the apparently identical virus, it kills the birds and it can be transmitted to man."

"And it can infect other birds."

"Yes, very easily, that's how it spread so quickly."

"Then the thing to find out now is if Rand-beta when transmitted to man becomes Rand-alpha. If it does our troubles are over. It will mean killing a lot of birds, but we can stop the disease at that stage and stop it from reinfecting human beings."

"That's what I'm hoping," she said, looking at the instruments attached to the bird's cage. "If the bird gets sick it will have Rand-beta, which means your patient has Rand-alpha—the same as the original case. It will prove that there are only two forms of the disease—and it can only be caught from birds. Once their reservoir of infection is wiped out that will be the end of it."

They both looked up as the pigeon, stretching out one wing, rolled onto its side.

"Its body temperature has gone up four degrees," Nita said.

The first boil formed and they saw that disease was following the now all too familiar course.

"I'll get a blood specimen down to the lab," Nita said, "to be checked with the electron microscope. But I don't think there is any doubt, do you?"

"None at all," he said as he took a hypodermic needle from the autoclave. "There is only one factor missing from the whole series to prove whether it's right or wrong." He turned toward the patient on the bed.

"No! You mustn't!" Nita shouted, running after him. She grabbed his arm so hard that the hypodermic was jarred from his hand and broke on the floor. He turned to face her, quietly, without anger.

"Sam, you mustn't, they were talking about that over at World Health; there were suggestions that they ask for volunteers, but it was decided to wait. It's too dangerous now, there's no need . . ."

"There is a need. Until it is proven that Rand-alpha can't be transmitted from one person to another we can't be sure that there won't be an epidemic. And as long as there is doubt about that I am—both of us are going to be trapped in this isolation ward. Someone will have to be inoculated with the Rand-alpha virus from the policeman here. Since I have already been exposed to Rand-alpha by Rand himself, I'm the logical volunteer. Any arguments?"

"I should——"

He smiled. "In this particular case, my dear Doctor, it is women and children last."

For a long moment she was silent, then she turned away and opened the autoclave. "I can't argue with you," she said. "Perhaps you are right, I don't know. In any case I can't stop you. But I'm the cytologist here and I'm not going to let any ham-handed intern give himself hepatitis or pyemia or anything like that." She took out a new hypodermic. "I take care of preparing it, right?"

"Right," he said, and turned back to his patient while she prepared the culture. He knew, without reasoning it out, that she would make no attempt to fool him and prepare an injection of sterile water or neutral plasma. This was too important. She might be a woman, very much of a woman and equipped with all the female feelings and emotions—but she was still a physician.

"All ready," she said.

33

He swabbed his arm himself, and when he saw her hesitate he took the hypodermic needle from her fingers, held it vertical for a moment and squeezed out a few drops, then plunged it matter of factly through his skin.

"The Rand-alpha virus didn't propagate in human tissue culture," Nita said, her hands clasped so tightly together that her fingertips were white, "so there is almost no chance that you will catch the disease." She was trying to reassure herself as much as him and he recognized the fact. It had been an abrupt change for her, to move in a single day from the quiet laboratory to this jarring contact with death.

"Little or no chance at all," he said. "Hadn't you better report to McKay what we have done while I take a look at the patient?"

The policeman was still asleep—but was his breathing hoarser? Sam thumbed the transcript button on the medical recorder and it whirred softly as it scanned the minute-to-minute record it had made of the patient's medical history since he had been placed in the bed. There was a clunk and the sheet of graph paper fell into Sam's hand. He followed the recorded curves of the different instruments and they all showed a steady deterioration up until the time of the interferon injection. At this point—almost three hours earlier —the decline leveled off, even improved slightly when the antipyretic brought the fever down. But the remission was over, the fever was rising again, blood pressure decreasing and the stricken man was sliding once more toward the threshold of death. Sam at once prepared another injection of interferon and administered it. It appeared to have no effect.

"Dr. McKay was very angry," Nita said. "Then he said that we must keep accurate account of what happens, he thinks you're an insane fool—I'm quoting—but he thanks you for doing it. Has there . . . been anything?" She turned his wrist so she could look at the dials of the telltale there.

"No, no reaction at all, you can see for yourself. There's no reason that there should be, human tissue culture is sensitive enough. If Rand-alpha were transmittable to human tissue we would know it by now."

Once more a patient of Dr. Bertolli was dying before his eyes and there was nothing he could do. The interferon had worked at first, delaying the onslaught by a few hours, but it would not work a second time. Higher and higher the fever rose and the antipyretic no longer affected it. The heart-lung machine was attached and then the artificial kidney when renal failure seemed imminent. Sam's only hope was that he could aid the patient's body in its fight against the invading virus, support it with transfusions of whole blood and stave off any secondary infections with antibiotics. It was a hopeless cause but he would not admit it. This was a battle he had to win, but he could not. Only when Nita pulled at his arm and he became aware that she was crying did he turn away.

"Sam, he's dead, please, there's nothing more you can do."

The exhaustion hit him then; how long had it been, twelve hours or more? He looked at his watch and noticed the telltale on his arm. It was registering normally, though his pulse was depressed with fatigue. He had forgotten all about it! If he were going to catch the virulent Rand's disease he would have had it by now; the experiment had paid off, he was safe. It seemed a small victory after the tragedy of the last hours.

"Sit down, please," she said, "and here's some black coffee." He sipped it first, then gulped at it, drinking almost the entire cup at once before he put it down.

"What's been happening?" he asked. "It's after two in the morning."

"We've been released from quarantine, that was Dr. McKay's decision. He said if there were no symptoms by midnight that the quarantine was over . . ." She put her hand on his arm as he started to rise. "Now wait, please, finish the coffee and hear the rest."

He hesitated a moment, then sat down heavily. "It's good coffee and I'll have another cup." He almost smiled. "I'm sorry if I have been acting like an idiot, but this whole dirty business has been so personal, ever since Rand came out of the ship, practically falling into our arms. Here, sit down, and have some coffee yourself."

She poured the coffee and stirred cream and sugar into hers.

"The city is in a very bad way," she said. "I can tell that from the medical reports. The Rand-beta virus is easy to pick up and deadly. The birds die very quickly after being infected, but by the time they do their entire body and all their feathers are coated with the virus. Apparently the virus spreads by simple contact with the skin, all of the people who have caught it have either handled a bird or touched the ground where the bird has been. The virus eventually dies after leaving the host, but they are not sure yet how long it takes."

"How many cases have there been?"

She hesitated a moment before she answered. "Over three thousand the last I heard."

"So fast!— What's being done?"

"So far just stopgap measures, but there is a meeting going on right now, all the medical authorities, the mayor, police, everyone, here in Bellevue in auditorium number two. Professor Chabel of World Health is the chairman and he wants you to come down. I saved that information for last because you looked like you needed the cup of coffee first."

"I did," he said, standing and stretching, more under control. Nita stood too, very close, and his hands went out, almost of their own volition, taking her by the shoulders. He started to say something but he was aware only of the warmth of her flesh through the thin cotton smock. Then he was pulling her closer and her lips were on his, firm and alive, her strong arms holding him tightly against her body.

"Well!" he said, more than a little surprised at himself. "I'm really not sure why I did that. I'm sorry . . ."

"Are you?" She was smiling. "Well, I'm not. I thought it was very nice. Though I imagine it would feel even better after you have shaven."

When he ran his fingers up his cheeks they rasped like sandpaper. "I hadn't realized it—I must look like a porcupine, I certainly feel like one. Before I go down to that meeting I'll have to get rid of these."

The strip lighting around the mirror in the bathroom threw back dazzling highlights from the glazed tile and polished metal fixtures, and Sam squinted at his features through the glare. The radiating head of the supersonic shaver moved smoothly over his skin, shattering the brittle whiskers, but was irritatingly audible when he pressed too hard over the bone. The shaver's sound was of course too high pitched to hear directly, but it vibrated his skull and set up overtones that whined in his inner ear like a fleet of tiny insects. His eyes were red-rimmed and set in darkened sockets. Aspirin would take care of the headache and five milligrams of Benzedrine would get him through the meeting, but he would have to stop by his room first and get some shoes; the white jacket and pants would be all right but he couldn't very well wear the cotton scuffs.

"Will you let me know what is going to happen?" Nita asked as he was leaving. He nodded as he pushed again, impatiently, on the door switch as it slowly began the opening cycle.

"Yes, I'll phone you as soon as I can," he said distractedly, thinking about the city outside. He would have to be prepared for a number of changes.

When the outer door finally opened after the sterilizing cycle and Sam stepped through, the first thing he saw was Killer Dominguez stretched out asleep on a bench outside. Killer opened one eye suspiciously when the door mechanism hummed, then jumped to his feet.

"Welcome back to civilization, Doc, for a while there we were afraid they were gonna throw away the key on you, but I got it on the grapevine that you were outta quarantine so I came along as a committee of one to offer congratulations."

"Thanks, Killer. Did the grapevine also tell you that I had to get right down to this meeting?"

"It did. And Charley Stein in the gyn lab said they would probably incinerate all your clothes. Including shoes? I asked, and he said no doubt of it." Killer reached under the bench and dragged out a pair of white, gum-soled shoes. "So I figured at least you oughta have a pair of shoes, so I got these out of your room, and I see I figured right."

"You're a friend in need, Killer," Sam said, kicking off the scuffs and zipping up the shoes. "You've been on duty while I've been locked up here—what's it like outside?"

For the first time since Sam had known him Killer's face lost its neutral expression of urban sophistication, falling into lines of fatigue and worry.

"It's rough, Doc—and it's gonna get rougher. Everyone's staying in the house with the doors locked but pretty soon they're gonna start getting low on food and figure the best thing to do is to visit the relatives in the country and then the fun'll start. The whole thing's being played down by the papers and TV, but you can read between the lines and I've seen some stuff myself—a riot on the East Side but nothing in the papers about it."

"I think we'll have it under control soon," Sam said as they went to the elevator, wishing he could put more sincerity into his words. "Once we've stopped the birds from spreading Rand's disease it will die out."

"There're a lot of birds in the world, Doc," Killer said, chewing idly on a toothpick, his accustomed unshakable expression back.

The entrance to auditorium number two was closed and guarded by an unsmiling policeman who refused Sam admittance and kept his hand on his belt near his gun while he talked. When he had been reassured that Sam did have business here he called on his helmet radio and a few minutes later Eddie Perkins, one of the resident surgeons, opened the door. Killer vanished and Eddie ushered Sam into the cloakroom.

"I have to brief you first," he said, "before you go in there. It's turning into a real battle."

"Whose side are you on?"

"You might as well ask." Eddie smiled crookedly and took out a pack of cigarettes and when Sam refused lit one himself. "I've been drafted with Dr. McKay's team. He's been officially placed in charge of the medical investigation and treatment for Rand's disease; everyone remembers what he did with Topholm's pachyacria. He throws some weight with the public health people, less with the police and military, and none at all with the vote-hungry politicians. He's trying to convince the governor that he should declare martial law so the UN Army can come in—we'll need them sooner or later, so it's better sooner—and at the same time we should destroy every bird within a hundred mile radius of New York."

"There must be hundreds of state parks and game sanctuaries in that area. I can imagine what the conservationists are going to say!"

"They've already said it—and to the governor, who you'll remember is up for reelection in the fall."

"What can I do about all this?"

"McKay says you can probably swing the vote the right way; he's been stalling until you showed up. You make an entrance and everyone will shut up and listen to what you have to say. You're the hero of the moment, the guy who first saw Rand and who went into quarantine with him, then took a dose of the bugs to prove that Rand-alpha is not communicable between human beings. Once that's shown to be true the panic about catching the disease will die down along with all the talk about evacuating the city, and it will stop the worry about quarantining the cases we have so far. Then once you establish the noncommunicability of Rand-alpha you have to say in a loud and clear voice that the only way Rand-beta can be stopped is by killing a few million birds. Do you agree?"

"I—yes, of course I do. It sounds like a horrible idea, but it is the only thing to do when we have no cure for the disease. Stop it now before it spreads and we'll have it stopped forever."

"That's the old fighting spirit," Perkins said as he started for the door. "Convince the ward heelers of that and we can get on with the job. Give me a two-minute start so I can tip off McKay, then bust in. Go right up to the platform, we'll be waiting for you."

They were slow minutes. Sam straightened his white jacket in the cloakroom mirror and tried to brush away some of the wrinkles. His throat was dry, just the way it used to be before a combat drop. Politicians! But they had to be convinced at once. Every minute's delay spread the circle of contamination further. He pushed through the door and went down the aisle of the partially filled hall toward the impressive group of uniforms and business suits seated around the long table on the platform. Heads turned toward him and Dr. McKay broke off his speech and greeted him.

"Now, gentlemen, we can at last have a few facts to deal with, incontrovertible facts and evidence on which we can base a logical decision. This is Dr. Bertolli, whom I think you all know by name."

A murmur rippled through the hall and Sam tried to ignore the staring eyes as he climbed the four steps to the stage. McKay waved him to his side.

"At the present moment Dr. Bertolli is the world's clinical authority on Rand's disease. He was the one who met Rand when the ship landed and attended his case in quarantine here, as well as the second case, that of Police Officer Miles. In addition he is the man who conducted the experiments that have just proven that we can only catch Rand's disease from birds, not from one another. Dr. Bertolli, will you tell us, what were the nature of these experiments?"

When McKay said this, Sam realized that the man was a shrewd politician as well as a physician. By not revealing the exact nature of the communicability tests he had set the stage for a dramatic revelation by Sam. Sam normally did not have much use for political doctors, but he realized that at this moment he would have to be one himself. His audience had to be convinced. There was an expectant silence as he turned to face them.

"Laboratory tests have revealed that Rand's disease appears to have two forms, called alpha and beta for identification. Commander Rand died of Rand-alpha, but it was impossible for him to infect any creature other than members of the class aves, birds, since any and all kinds of birds apparently can catch this disease from man. When the birds become infected the disease becomes Rand-beta, a virulent form that can be passed on to other birds or to human beings. However, when man catches it, it appears as Rand-alpha again—this is what Officer Miles died of. This disease can not be communicated to others."

"How do you know, Doctor?" McKay interrupted.

"Because I injected myself with the live virus taken from Miles."

Sam broke off as a concerted gasp ran through the audience; those at the table nearest him inadvertently leaned away. McKay had a cold smile as he put his hand on Sam's arm.

"There is no need to be alarmed. If Dr. Bertolli were to have contracted the disease he would have the obvious symptoms by now; it has been observed that all of the cases now under treatment developed within one hour of exposure." He dropped his arm and sat back in his chair, looking directly at Sam, who stood alone, facing the silent audience. "Do you have any more suggestions for the treatment of Rand's disease, Doctor?"

"None," Sam said, then let the silence stretch. "As of this present moment the disease is incurable. Anyone who contracts it will die. The only way to prevent it will be to wipe out the reservoirs of infection, to kill every bird within ten miles of New York City, or twenty miles or a hundred or a thousand, whatever is needed to make sure that not a single bird escapes. I know this is a shocking idea, but there is no alternative. To put it very simply—it is the birds or us."

There were a number of angry shouts, which Dr. McKay

ignored, almost turning his back so he would not have to notice the red-faced governor of New York State, who had sprung to his feet.

"We have one person here who is qualified to tell us what must be done, Professor Burger, curator of the New York Zoological Park. Professor Burger . . ."

Burger was a slight man with a pink, bald head covered by a few carefully placed strands of white hair. He spoke with his face lowered and he was difficult to hear until the hall grew quiet.

". . . patterns of flight and normal roosting and homing behavior of various species. I have worked out the maximum area of possible infection, representing, we might say, a diseased bird of one of the more free-ranging species being infected and flying until unable to continue, then infecting another and so forth. I would therefore say——" He shuffled through the papers before him and a muttering grew in the audience. "I beg your indulgence, gentlemen," he said, raising his head, and it could be seen that his eyes were wet and tears marked his cheeks. "I have just come from the zoo, where we have killed, poisoned all of our birds, all of them —yes, here are the figures. A radius from Manhattan of one hundred miles in all directions, slightly more on Long Island to take in Montauk Point, should be satisfactory. Though this area may have to be extended depending on later reports."

"That's impossible," someone shouted. "That will be an area of nearly ten thousand square miles, it would take an army!"

"It will need the Army," Burger said. "The UN Army must be called on for help. It will need gas, poison bait, shotguns, explosives . . ."

Slowly, through the following uproar, Professor Chabel's gavel could be heard, banging for attention. He continued until his voice could be heard.

"This is a problem of World Health, which is why I was selected to chair this meeting. I believe we have heard all that is necessary to make a decision and I call for an immediate vote."

There were more complaints at this which died away even more slowly. The vote, when it was finally counted, was no landslide, but the effective measures had been passed. The Army would move in and the slaughter would begin at dawn.

41

6

"I saw on TV where the beach on Coney Island was covered with dead seagulls, washed up during the night, so they closed the whole beach off not that anyone is breaking their neck to go swimming anyway."

Killer talked around his half-chewed toothpick while he drove, tooling the big ambulance down the center of the deserted crosstown street. All the cars were parked and locked and there were no pedestrians in sight.

"Slow down," Sam said. "Remember we're cruising and not on the way to a ruptured appendix." He was sitting on the right, looking into all the doorways and areaways that they passed. So far he had seen nothing. It was crowded on the front seat with the three of them there. The third man was a UN soldier named Finn, a tall Dane bulking like a pack mule in his full field equipment and forced to lean forward because of the flamethrower on his back.

"There under—under the car," the soldier broke in suddenly, pointing at a delivery truck. "I think I saw something there." They braced themselves as Killer hit the brakes and squealed to a stop.

Sam was first out, shouldering the emergency bag as he went; the contents of this bag was one of the measures that had been outlined at the meeting the previous evening.

Finn had good eyes. The dark shadow huddled against the rear wheel of the truck was a young man who tried to crawl further under when they approached. Sam knelt down and, even in the bad light, he could see the characteristic flushed skin and incipient boils of Rand's disease. He took a pair of elbow-length isolation gloves from the bag and pulled them on.

"Let me help you out from there," he told the sick man, but when he reached under the man scrambled further away, eyes wide with fear. Sam grabbed his leg, warded off one feeble kick, then slowly pulled him out into the street. The man struggled briefly, then the whites of his eyes rolled up as he passed out: this would make handling him a good deal easier.

The gas mask was an ordinary can respirator type from the fire department stocks, and had been modified quickly by coating the inside with a biocidal cream. When Sam had seated this firmly on the patient's face he took a pressurized container of antiseptic from his bag and soaked the man's clothes and skin, then rolled him onto his side so he could do his back. Only then did he strip off the gloves and begin treatment, sure that any Rand-beta virus on his skin or clothing had been killed. He took off the gas mask and prepared an injection of interferon, still the only treatment that had any effect on the disease. The UN soldier came back and stood frowning down at them and fingering the handpiece of his flamethrower.

"There are no birds near here, none; I searched very carefully. Have you asked him where he could have touched a bird?"

"He's unconscious, I didn't have a chance."

Killer had backed the ambulance up and opened the rear door, then wheeled out the stretcher. He tilted his head to one side and the other, frowning down at the unconscious man's face.

"Don't he look sort of Italian to you, Doc?"

"He could be—but what difference would that make?"

"Maybe nothing, but you know there's plenty of pigeon fanciers in this neighborhood, racers and homing pigeons, and a lot of them are Italian. They keep hutches on the roofs."

They both looked up automatically as he said it, just in time to see a flick of white on the edge of the parapet high above.

"No—not my birds, didn't have anything to do with my birds . . ." The sick man shouted, trying to struggle to his feet.

Sam ripped the end off a riot shot—a disposable, one-shot hypodermic of powerful sedative that was self-powered by a cartridge of compressed gas—and pressed it to the struggling man's arm. It hissed slightly and the patient fell back, unconscious.

"Roll him onto the stretcher and get him into the ambulance. Finn and I will see what's on the roof."

Killer protested. "You could use me there to——"

"I could use you here to watch the patient a lot better. On the job, Killer."

43

They went as far as the top floor in the elevator, then headed toward the stairs, the soldier first. Doors slammed shut as they approached and they knew that they were being watched all the way. At the head of the stairs was the roof door, closed and sealed with a large padlock.

"The rights of private property must always be observed," Finn observed gloomily, rattling the lock. "However, paragraph fourteen of our emergency commission reads . . ." The rest of his words were drowned out as he raised his steel-shod, size-fifteen boot and kicked hard against the lock. Screws squealed as they tore from the frame and the door swung open.

Ahead of them stood a large and freshly painted dovecote above which two pigeons were circling. Clearly visible on the floor inside were a dozen more lying on their sides, some feebly beating their wings.

"What is this floor made of?" the soldier asked, stamping his foot on the roof. Sam looked down at it.

"This is a new building so it must be one of the asbestos slurryes."

"They are fireproof?" Finn asked, opening a valve on his tank.

"Yes, of course."

"Very good." He raised the flamethrower, waiting for the birds in the air to settle. They were disturbed by the strangers and by the sick birds lying below. The soldier watched steadily, nozzle pointed and his finger on the trigger, until all of the birds were down at the same time. He squeezed the trigger.

A roaring tongue of flame licked over the dovecote changing it from inert wood to a burning framework in an instant. One of the birds was caught in the air, a burning puff of fire that crashed to the roof.

"You're murderers!" the young woman screeched as she came through the door behind them. She tried to clutch at Finn but Sam took her arms and held her immobile until she burst into tears and sagged against him. He let her slide down to the doorstep and touched her wrist lightly with his tell-tale. No, she didn't have Rand's disease, she was just one of the unfortunate bystanders so far. Perhaps the man in the ambulance was her husband.

There was a bubbling hiss as Finn sprayed the roof and the burning framework with his chemical fire extinguisher. While he kicked the smoking debris aside to make sure the flames were out he talked into his helmet radio, then rejoined Sam.

"I've reported in and they will send a decontamination team up here. We can go." He was young, Sam realized, and was trying very hard not to look at the girl sobbing on the step.

When they came out of the building Killer had the ambulance waiting in front of the entrance with the car door open and the turbine throbbing.

"They got a riot," he called out, "up by the Queens Midtown Tunnel entrance; it's outta our district but they need all the help they can get. Dispatcher said to get up there."

As usual Killer did his best to make the ponderous ambulance perform like a racing car, thundering it north on Park Avenue, then swinging into Twentieth Street. They drove with the windows closed, as ordered, and the odor of burned fuel was strong in the cab. When they passed Gramercy Park a decontamination team in sealed plastic suits was raking up the corpses of dead birds: a shotgun thudded under the trees and a tumbled ball of black feathers dropped to the ground.

"Poison grain, that's what they been spreading," Killer said, swinging into Third Avenue and pressing hard on the accelerator. "That gets most of them, and what the poison don't get the shotguns do. It's a real mess—— Hey, look up ahead!"

A jam of unmoving cars filled the street, most of them empty now: two of them had crashed together and burned. A motorcycle policeman waved them over to the curb and leaned in the rolled-down window.

"They got some casualties down the plaza by the entrance at Thirty-sixth. You know where it is?" Killer flared his nostrils in silent contempt at this doubting question. "It's quieter now, but keep your eyes open." He pointed to the soldier's flamethrower. "You got a weapon besides that thing?" he asked.

"I am fully armed, Officer." Finn swiveled in the seat and his recoilless .50 appeared in his hand.

"Yeah, well don't point it at me, just keep it handy. There's been trouble down here and there could be more. Take this tank up on the sidewalk, there's room enough to get through."

This was the kind of driving Killer enjoyed. He bumped up the curb and rolled down the sidewalk toward the plaza. There was the sound of shouting ahead, and racing motors,

45

followed by a tremendous crash of breaking glass. A man ran around the corner toward them, his arms clutching a load of liquor bottles. When he saw the approaching ambulance he ran out in the street to go around it.

"A looter!" Killer said, curling his lip in disgust.

"He's not our responsibility——" Sam said, then broke off as the man came closer. "Wait, stop him!"

Killer did this efficiently by throwing his door open just as the man was trying to pass. There was a thud and the crash of breaking bottles, then the ambulance braked to stop. They were so close to the wall that Sam had to vault the hood, jumping down by the fallen man who was on all fours, shaking his head in a welter of broken glass and spilled whiskey. Sam bent to look at his face then stepped back, pulling on isolation gloves.

"Stay in the cab," he shouted. "He has it, an advanced case."

Sam was looking into his bag, taking out a riot shot, and when he glanced up the broken bottle was coming down toward his face and Killer was howling a warning from the cab. It was a trained reflex that raised his arm to stop the blow, his forearm striking at the other's wrist. The man was weak—how could he walk at all riddled with the cysts as he must be?—and could only swing again feebly. Sam kept a tight grip on the man's wrist while he slapped him in the back of the neck with a riot shot. The stricken man began to sag at once and Sam had to drag him clear of the broken glass before he could let him fall to the ground. As swiftly as possible he adminstered the interferon shot and the prescribed antiseptic treatment. Killer had the upper bunk swung down and locked and Finn helped him swing the inert body up into it. When they moved forward again the UN soldier walked in front of the ambulance.

They could not reach Second Avenue because the crush of cars had pressed up onto the sidewalk and against the buildings there. Sam unshipped two of the lightweight magnesium stretchers and the emergency kit and, fully loaded, twisted his way behind the alert soldier toward the plaza by the tunnel entrance.

The riot was over and had left behind a score of wounded and dead. An airborne UN medical team had arrived with the soldiers in a big combat copter; it had landed in the roadway just before the tunnel entrance, and they were already tending the wounded. A blood-soaked policeman lay on the ground next to his patrol car and the drip in his arm led to the plasma bottle hung from the car's rearview mirror. The soldiers had moved in quickly and aided the police in rounding up those of the battered rioters who had not escaped. Separated from the jam of the other cars was a still smoking and flame-seared panel truck. A police lieutenant near it saw Sam's white jacket and waved him over.

"Anything to be done with this one, Doctor?" He pointed to the man crumpled on the front seat of the truck whose hand, spotted with dried blood, hung out of the window. Sam put down his burdens and pressed the telltale against the projecting wrist. Temperature seventy-eight, no pulse.

"He's dead." Sam put the instrument back into its case. "What happened here?"

"Just a crowd at first. We're trying to control all traffic to the Island because most of the cases of plague are still coming from there. Make sure people live there or got business, and stop them from taking any birds out. That's what set it off. There was a lot of horn-blowing and shouting, but nothing else until someone saw the sign PET SHOP on this truck and hauled the doors open. This poor slob had it full of birds from his shop, God knows what he thought he was doing with them. Someone shot him, they set the truck on fire, then they spotted a couple of guys with plague and after that I lost track until the Army arrived . . ."

"Doctor—over here!" Finn was waving and Sam saw that he was pointing to two men lying on a cleared patch of ground. They both had Rand's disease. He began the prophylaxis and treatment at once.

Maximum capacity of the ambulance was eight and they had only four cases of Rand's disease, but all of the conscious burn and wound cases refused to travel in the same machine. There was no point in arguing, so they carried in the unconscious policeman with the plasma drip and left the last three places empty. Killer backed skillfully up the street and, with siren wailing, they rushed back to Bellevue. On the way they received a radioed warning that the emergency wards were full and the operating rooms jammed: they went around to the main entrance, where volunteer stretcher-bearers from the clerical departments were waiting to carry the patients up to the just-evacuated maternity wards. The hospital was rapidly being filled to capacity.

Sam was refilling his depleted emergency kit in the supply room when Tomo Miletich, another intern, found him.

"Sign here and here," Tomo said, pushing a hospital form over to him. "I'm taking over your meat wagon and you're supposed to call telephone central for a message. Is Killer your driver?"

"Yes, he's at the wheel." Sam scrawled his initials. "But what is it about?"

"No idea, I just follow orders. See you—if I survive Killer's driving." He shouldered the refilled kit and left. Sam looked for a phone.

"Just a moment, Dr. Bertolli," the operator said, and flicked through her message file. "Yes, there is a guest in your room who is waiting for you, and after this will you please see Professor Chabel, he's with Dr. McKay in 3911." /

"Do you know who is waiting in my room?"

"There is no record of that, Doctor."

"Yes, well, thank you." He hung up and rubbed his jaw, wondering. What was this all about? Who could be important enough to take him away from the emergency work? And how were Chabel and World Health involved? He started to call first, then decided it would be better to go right up. The only stop he made was to wash some of the soot from his hands and face before he pushed open the unlocked door to his room.

It was an UN Army officer, a big man whose back was turned as he stood looking out of the window with his hands clasped behind him in the position of parade rest. His garrison hat was on the table and the peak was rich with gold braid, a field officer. Sam's eyes jumped from the hat to the familiar hand-tooled holster hanging from the officer's belt, out of which projected the chrome-and-teak butt of a recoilless .75. As the man turned Sam's shoulders squared automatically and he had to resist the desire to throw a salute.

"It's been ten years, hasn't it, Sam?" General Burke asked, swinging about and sticking out a large and gnarled brown hand. Sam took it and remembered just in time to clamp down hard with his fingers so that they wouldn't get crushed.

"Yes, sir, at least ten years," Sam answered. He could think of nothing better to say. Burke looked the same, perhaps a few more crowfeet at the corner of those burning, dark eyes, maybe a little more thrust to that big jaw. But what was he doing here?

"Listen, Sam, I won't call you doctor if you won't call me sir, or general." He gave a last powerful contraction before he let go of Sam's hand. "My friends call me Cleaver."

"I was there when you got the name," Sam said, and he had to smile as he did. It was during the evacuation operation on Formosa. There had been a night guerrilla raid while all of the officers had been in the mess tent and, for one of the rare times in his life, General Burke hadn't been armed. But he had grabbed a meat cleaver from the cook and howling like an Indian—thereby giving new strength to the rumor that he was half Apache—had chopped a hole in the side of the tent and fallen on the guerrillas from the rear. It was a night that was hard to forget—especially for Sam, who had been the rawest second lieutenant in the company.

"By Christ, I had forgotten that, you were a crummy shavetail then, but you learned fast enough." Sam was expecting the slap on the back so he swung with it so that his shoulder blade wasn't fractured.

"Cleaver" Burke had a big mouth, big muscles and at times seemed to be a parody of the perfect Texan. He was also one of the shrewdest field officers in the Army and did nothing without a purpose.

"What are you here for, Cleaver? It can't be just to renew an old acquaintance?"

"Right from the shoulder like always, hey, Sam? Pour me a drink of something and I'll lay it on the line."

There was an open bottle of Irish whisky in the closet and Sam, remembering Cleaver's tastes, found a water glass and filled it half full. He hesitated until he remembered he would be off duty for a while, then poured one for himself.

"Here's to the Irish, their bogs and their whisky," General Burke said, holding up his glass.

"Uisce beathadh."

Burke drained most of it with a single swallow, then frowned at the empty glass before he put it down. "This plague from space is the biggest trouble you or I have seen in our time, Sam, and it's going to get worse before it's better. I need your help."

"There's not much that I can do, Cleaver. I'm out of the Army and busy doctoring."

"I know, and I'll let you go back to work as soon as we're finished, but I need some more information. You were there when Rand came out, you talked to him, you watched him write that message. Do you have any idea what he meant by it—or why he sealed the ship after he left?"

"Just what I've put into the reports. I did the postmortem

and I've been thinking about it since then. You can't put too much meaning into what he wrote, one way or the other."

"What do you mean——?"

"Without being too clinical, let's say his brain was affected. He was barely conscious, with a high fever and his blood stream loaded with toxins. What he wrote about sickness in the ship might have been a terribly important message, or just the meandering of a damaged mind."

General Burke was pacing the room, his anachronistic spurs clinking with each footstep. He wheeled about and glared at Sam.

"But this is just guesswork, you don't know one way or the other. What about the 'Pericles'? When you made the phone calls, didn't you see anything unusual, anyone else, bodies, signs of violence? Anything?"

"Just what I reported, Cleaver. I wouldn't know a real spaceship from a TV stage setting. What I saw looked in order, and there was no one visible in any of the compartments. But this should be easy enough to check; someone could get into the air lock with a camera and dial the numbers as I did and record the whole thing."

"Sounds easy enough when you put it that way. But it's very hard to take pictures through a half inch of steel."

"What do you mean——?"

"I mean that old maid Chabel at World Health is so afraid of contamination that he has had a steel plate welded over the lock opening and he won't permit it to be removed to investigate the lock or to take the pictures you just mentioned."

"You can't very well blame him, considering what happened when that air lock was opened once before. That and Rand's warning. Until we learn more about Rand's disease the wisest thing to do is to leave the ship alone."

General Burke's hair almost crackled with electricity when he brushed his hand angrily across it. "Maybe. And maybe again there are records in that ship about how they got the disease and who died of it and maybe how to fight it. There has to be something written there, and anything would be a help."

"And there might be even worse infections there, which is why Rand sealed the lock behind him. If there were any records of importance he could have put them in his pockets before he landed, after all he was conscious enough to bring that ship home and set her down in one piece. You can argue this either way, Cleaver, and both answers make as much sense. As a last resort I might agree with you, if everything were going wrong. Open it up, we couldn't be worse off. But we're getting Rand's disease under control. It can only be caught from birds as you know, so we're wiping them out. Once the source of infection is removed we'll be rid of Rand's disease."

"I know all about the damned birds, that's why I'm here. I have my HQ in Fort Jay, but my division is out with shotguns and birdlime and butterfly nets, stumbling all over Long Island killing birds. They'll do a good job, I'll see to that, but it's no way to fight a war. We need intelligence and what we need to know is in that ship. I'm asking for your help, Sam. After what you've done people respect what you say. If you said let's take a quick peek into the ship there would be enough pressure on old Chabel so that he would have to relent. What do you say, son?"

Sam stared into his glass, spinning the amber liquid around and around. "I'm sorry, Cleaver. I wish I could help you, but I can't. Not this time. You see I agree with Chabel."

"That the last word, Sam?" Burke stood and put his hat under his arm.

"That's it, Cleaver."

"Well you're wrong, son, and being bullheaded, but I can't hold it against a man for sticking to his guns. But you think on it and when you change your mind come right to me." He crushed Sam's hand in his and turned to the door.

"I'll think on it, Cleaver—but until there's some new evidence I'm not going to change my mind."

The door slammed and Sam grinned wryly and wriggled his numbed fingers. Ten years hadn't slowed Cleaver down in the slightest. He finished his drink and pulled a clean suit of hospital whites from the drawer. He had a better idea now why Chabel wanted to see him.

Dr. McKay's secretary had Sam wait before she let him into the office, and when she finally opened the door for him he walked into a silence: McKay sitting behind his wide desk and Professor Chabel puffing his pipe silently in the corner. Sam knew they had been talking about him, and he would find out why quickly enough.

"You sent for me, Dr. McKay?"

"Yes, Sam, I—and Professor Chabel—wanted to talk to you. There, pull up a chair and make yourself comfortable." McKay rattled the papers on his desk and looked unhappy.

Sam grinned a bit as he sat down in the chair and McKay's darting glance caught it, and he was a good enough diagnostician to read the correct meaning into it.

"All right, Sam, no beating around the bush then. We arranged for that buzzard Burke to see you, we thought it would be better that way, get it out in the open. He wanted you to help him, didn't he?"

"Yes, he did."

There was tension in the room now and, without realizing it, Chabel rocked forward in his chair.

"What did you tell him?"

"I told him that I couldn't help him, and I told him why. As the situation stands now I feel that our decision, Professor Chabel, in sealing up the spaceship was a correct one. I don't see how we could gain anything by opening it up, and we could lose a great deal."

"I'm very pleased to hear that, Dr. Bertolli," Chabel said, leaning back in his chair as he pushed the dottle in his pipe down with his thumb. He tipped in fresh tobacco. "We have enough trouble battling Rand's disease, but we would be in twice as much difficulty if we had to fight General Burke at the same time. The general is a tenacious man, which makes him a wonder in the field of battle, but he also wishes to have a hand in policy making. He is far too wise to act without aid, and so far he represents only a small group of extremists who wish to enter the 'Pericles,' and up until now the news agencies have cooperated with us in seeing that they don't get their views into print. However, this would all change if they had some popular figure on their side—such as yourself. If that happened we couldn't keep this intramural battle under the table, and I don't feel that at the present time we can enjoy the luxury of a policy debate in public. The situation is too desperate for that."

"Desperate——?" Sam asked, surprised. "I had the feeling that things were getting under control."

"Temporarily, and only here in the city. But we are running into immense difficulties in both controlling the movement of the population and in bird extermination. There is no safe agent that will kill only birds nor one that is one hundred percent effective. We have had to push our outer circle back already because of breakthroughs of infection. The human element is difficult; we have had armed resistance from poultry farmers when we have attempted to kill off their entire flocks. They find it hard to see a connection between their healthy birds and a human disease eighty miles away. And then we have the factor of human fear. Enough people have seen cases of Rand's disease to know that it is striking all around them, and it appears to be common knowledge now that it is one hundred percent fatal. People are trying to leave the contaminated zone by stealth, or violence if there is no other way, and we have been forced to retaliate with violence—we have had no choice. This plague *must* be confined physically until we have developed some form of treatment." He looked automatically toward Dr. McKay as he said this, as did Sam.

"Has the research turned up anything?" Sam asked in the embarrassed silence that followed.

McKay shook his head *no* with his hands clasped on the desk before him: because they were trembling, Sam realized suddenly. McKay had a dreadful responsibility.

"We have a number of teams working around the clock, but we have accomplished next to nothing so far. We can describe the development of the disease better now, we know the first symptoms appear within thirty minutes of exposure, and we have developed supportive techniques that affect the advance of the disease, but they only slow it. We have not reversed one case yet. And there are a growing number of cases all the time.

"So you see, we have more than enough problems as things stand. General Burke represents just one more difficulty that we are not equipped to cope with."

"I would like to ask your help in another way, Sam," McKay broke in.

"Anything, of course."

"I could use you on my team. We're trying everything possible to break through on Rand's disease, and we need all the help we can get. You'd be an asset, Sam."

Sam hesitated a moment, trying to frame his words exactly before he spoke. "I don't envy you your job, Dr. McKay, even with the help you have. You must have pathologists, virologists, internists, epidemiologists, cytologists—all the best people in every field working with you. I, well, would be out of place with them. By chance I was there when Rand left the ship and later I was the best guinea pig handy to try the Rand-alpha virus on. But that's all. I'm an intern and I hope to be an experienced surgeon some day—but right now I think I'm most valuable in the back of an ambulance. Thank you for asking me, but I think I would just be a—dead weight with your people."

Chabel puffed on his pipe, saying nothing, and McKay smiled wryly. "Thanks, Sam, for going so easy with an old man. I really would like you on my team, aside from the obvious political fact that I would prefer you there rather than backing General Burke. But I'm not going to force you. God knows there is enough work out there for all of us and more." His intercom hummed and he switched it on. "Yes, of course," he said into it. "Send her in."

They were standing and saying good-by when Nita Mendel entered with a sheaf of papers. She stopped at the door.

"I can wait if you're busy, Dr. McKay," she said.

"No, that's fine, just leave them here. I want to go over these with Professor Chabel."

They went out of the office together and Sam said, "Coffee—or better yet, some food. I've missed some meals."

"I bet it won't be as good as the coffee we had in our private suite up there in quarantine."

They both smiled at the memory, nothing more; there was nothing more they could do, here in this place, at this time. Sam recognized the feelings he had—then turned his back on them. The world now was too upside down to allow him to consider personal desires. They took the elevator to the staff cafeteria.

"It's good soup," Nita said, taking small and precise spoonfuls.

"And cheap, too, very important for starving interns. Was there anything new in those reports, Nita, anything not classified that is?"

"No, not classified, but not for the public either. The hospitals report eight thousand cases in Manhattan alone, twenty-five thousand more in the other boroughs and the suburban area. The Army has commandeered a lot of hotels for emergency use; there aren't enough medical staff or supplies to care for them all, though volunteers are pouring in."

Sam pushed his half-finished bowl of soup away and stood up.

"I'm going to have to get back on the job—I had no idea it was that bad . . ."

He broke off as he picked his name from the string of half-heard messages from the loudspeaker on the table.

". . . for Dr. Bertolli. Will you please report to Dr. McKay's office. This is urgent. Dr. Bertolli . . ."

He went there as fast as he could without running, and pushed the door open to find both McKay and Chabel staring at a thin strip of paper.

"I think this is something you can do, Sam," McKay said, smiling as he held out the paper. "There's been a report from Orange County, from a GP up there. He's been treating a case of Rand's disease and he says that he has effected a cure."

7

The green and white police copter had landed on the copter port on the twenty-fifth floor setback and the door was open, waiting for Sam when he came out of the elevator. A police sergeant, a Negro with skin almost as dark as his uniform, an old New Yorker, stood in the doorway. He jumped down and helped Sam load in his medical kit, then slammed the door. The jets at the tips of the long copter blades began to whistle and the floor shuddered with their acceleration as the machine hauled itself into the air, swung in a tight arc and headed north. Once they were airborne the sergeant dropped into a seat and watched the rooftops of Manhattan stream by below. The vertical slabs of the midtown business section gave way to the grass- and tree-dotted residential areas, then the blue of the big lake in Harlem Park that had been blasted out of the heart of the old slum area. Just north of the park the silvery threads of the East and West Side monorail lines met and crossed. When the copter swung out in a wide arc over the Hudson River the sergeant turned away from the window and looked at Sam.

"You're Dr. Bertolli," he said, "and the commissioner himself told me I was to take you up to this spot in Orange County and bring you back in one piece. He didn't say why —is it still top secret?"

"No," Sam said, "I imagine he was just afraid of rumors

getting started before we found out the truth. But there is supposed to be a patient up there, the local doctor says he has cured him of Rand's disease . . ."

"The plague from space?" the pilot said, half turning his head to listen. "You catch it you're dead, every time, that's what I heard."

Sam caught the sergeant's eye and the big policeman smiled and shrugged. "The pilot's name is Forson, and in addition to having big ears he has a big mouth and he is a lousy pilot, but I understand he was born back there in the sticks where we are going so we'll need him."

"For a city slicker you got a lot to learn, Sarge," the pilot said, lifting the copter as they passed above the towers of the George Washington Bridge. "That's just my country-boy curiosity that made me listen in on your top-level conversation. Someday I'll be a sergeant and chew out the help too. Is that straight, Doc, about there being a guy that was cured?"

"That's what we're going there to find out." Sam looked at the two policemen, doing their job with quiet efficiency, and decided that telling the truth was the wisest course. "So far there is no cure for Rand's disease; if someone gets it he dies. So you can realize the importance of this. We have to find the right place and bring the patient and the doctor out."

"Know that country like the back of my hand," the pilot said, his face immobile, his eyes invisible behind the large sunglasses. "I come from Stony Point, great historical spot where we licked the British, and I've been all over those woods up there. I'll drop you right into the center of Stonebridge."

"Don't drop us, land us," the sergeant said coldly.

"A figure of speech, Sarge, that's all it was. I'll take you to the town, then all we have to do is find the right house."

At Haverstraw they turned away from the river and flew over the tree-covered slopes and the holiday lakes, all deserted now.

"Coming up," Forson said. "That's 17A below and the next turnoff leads up to Stonebridge; the farmhouse could be anywhere along the road here."

Dropping lower, the copter swung into a course above the narrow side road and followed it toward a cluster of buildings that was visible ahead. There were no cars on the road, and even the sidewalks in the center of town were empty.

They passed over it and when they reached the outskirts, on the far side, they saw a thread of smoke rising from beyond a grove of trees.

"That could be it," the pilot said, tapping the typewritten message taped above the control panel. "Says here farm near Stonebridge and a fire will be burning so we can find it by the smoke . . ."

As they cleared the stand of silver birches they had a clear view of the smoking remains of a farmhouse and barn. A few cows and chickens ran wildly when the copter appeared, but there were no human figures.

"I don't like the looks of this," the sergeant said. "That house is still smoldering and there's no one around. I wonder if it's the one we want?"

"No way of telling from up here," Forson said, tilting the machine into a tight circle. "Want to go down or swing around the town first?"

The animals had fled and the clearing around the farmhouse was still deserted.

"Around the town first, nothing much moving here and we can always come back. All right with you, Doctor?"

"Of course. There doesn't seem to be anything that we can do here and there is no indication that it is the house we are looking for."

"Up ahead, more smoke," the pilot said as they passed west of the settlement. He followed a rutted farm road to a clearing where a white, frame house stood. A man was in the yard waving up at them and a trickle of smoke rose from the chimney.

"This looks more like it," the sergeant said. He squinted into the sun as they turned and automatically loosened his recoilless .50 in its holster. "Is there enough room to set down there?"

"Enough room to put down five of these jobs. Here we go."

The man below took shelter in the doorway of the farm as the copter settled straight down, a billowing circle of dust and weeds blowing out from below it. They touched gently and rocked on the wheels: Sam reached for the door handle but the sergeant put his hand on his shoulder.

"I think I'll go out first, Doctor. The town was too quiet, and that house that burned down—there's just the smell of trouble around here. Stay here and keep an eye on the bus, Forson."

The pilot clicked off the jets and nodded. "You're just not used to the country, Sarge. It's always quiet like this." He grunted. "Why do you think I came to the city?"

The sergeant jumped down and walked slowly toward the man who came out of the farmhouse and waved again, a gray-haired man who wore old-fashioned suspenders over a white shirt.

"Come in," he called out. "I'm Dr. Stissing. I'm the one who called up; the patient is inside."

The sergeant gave him a quick look in passing and just nodded, then went into the house. He came out a few moments later and called across to the copter.

"This is the right place, there's a man in bed here."

Sam was waiting with his black bag and climbed down. Stissing looked a little bewildered, rubbing at the white stubble on his jaw. In his late seventies, Sam guessed. He shook hands.

"I'm Dr. Bertolli, Bellevue Hospital. I'd like to see your patient if I may."

"Yes, Doctor, of course. Right through there. I'm very glad to see you, very glad indeed; I've been up two days and a night and I'm not used to doing that any more. But Hadley in there phoned me, very frightened, and he should have been, because I recognized Rand's disease when I walked in and he knew himself that he had it. I've been treating him here alone ever since, and I have the fever licked and he's on the mend . . ."

"Do you mind if I have that curtain opened?" Sam asked. The room was dark and the man on the bed only a dim outline.

"Surely, of course, just resting Hadley's eyes."

The sergeant pulled up the curtain and Sam stood next to the bed, looking down at the middle-aged man with the red boils on his face: he put the telltale against his wrist.

"How are you feeling, Mr. Hadley?" he asked.

"Hadley's my first name. And I felt a whole lot better in my time, I tell you. Felt worse until the doc came."

Sam opened Hadley's pajama jacket—there were one or two boils scattered on his chest—then palpated his armpits: the lymph nodes were swollen.

"That hurts," Hadley said.

"Don't worry, you'll be all right."

"Then he is cured," Dr. Stissing said, his words tumbling

58

one over the other. "I knew it, I told him, these new antibiotics. The plague, I mean Rand's disease . . ."

"Hadley's a lucky man," Sam said tiredly, "he never had Rand's disease. This is common furunculosis complicated by a lympathic infection which the antibiotics have brought under control."

"But Rand's disease, the symptoms, the fever, all the same. I've been practicing long enough. . ."

"How long have you been ill, Hadley?" Sam asked.

"Couple of days. Fever hit me right after the rocket landed, like I told the doc. Felt like I was dying."

"That was the fever part—but how long have you had the boils?"

"Came at the same time. Of course I felt them coming on a few days earlier. Then the fever hit and I knew I had the plague . . ."

"Not the plague from space, Hadley," Dr. Stissing said, sitting down heavily on the wooden kitchen chair by the head of the bed. "Just a bad case of the boils. Boils and a fever. I'm . . . sorry, Doctor, about getting you up here from the city——"

The sudden crackle of small arms fire sounded from outside the house, from the front, broken by the heavy boom of a recoilless handgun. The sergeant ran from the room, drawing his pistol as he went; Sam was right behind him.

"Stay here!" Sam shouted over his shoulder to the bewildered doctor. He reached the parlor just as the sergeant threw open the front door. A hail of small arms fire splintered the door frame and punched holes in the floor. Sam had been under fire before, often enough to have developed all the correct instincts: he dived and rolled at the same time, out of the line of fire through the door. The sergeant lay crumpled in the doorway, his fingers still outstretched toward the bulk of the recoilless pistol, which lay on the porch outside. A few more shots splattered around the door as Sam grabbed him by the leg and pulled him away from the opening. The right shoulder of his uniform was spotted with blood and Sam tore it open: there was the entrance hole where a small-caliber bullet had penetrated. It must have been a magnum because the hydrostatic shock had knocked the sergeant out and, as Sam rolled him over to look at the exit wound, also small and bleeding only slightly, the sergeant opened his eyes and tried to sit up. Sam pressed him back.

"Take it easy—you've been hit."

"The hell you say!" The sergeant pushed Sam's hand away and struggled to a sitting position. "What's happening out there?"

Sam looked quickly from the side of the window, shielded by a curtain, and pulled his head back before the shots crashed through the glass. It was long enough for him to see the dark forms of the men who were running toward the copter, and to see the body of the pilot hanging halfway out of the doorway.

"Don't try nothing!" A voice called from outside. "You don't shoot at us and we're not going to shoot at you." Sam rose behind the curtain and the sergeant struggled up next to him. The men had pushed the limp pilot to the ground and were climbing in. One of them, the one who had been talking, held a young girl by the arms, shielding himself behind her body. She was in her twenties and the way her head hung and the way her clothing was torn left no doubt as to what had happened to her.

"Try anything I'll shoot the girl," the man shouted. "So help me I'll kill her. We don't want no more trouble, we just want to get away from the plague. Andy here can fly your whirly, learned in the Army, and we're going to take it and get out. Be smart and no one's going to get hurt."

He walked backward toward the door, dragging the girl with him. The jets whistled to life and the big blades began to move, faster and faster. When the copter began to rock on its landing gear the man in the doorway hurled the girl from him and climbed quickly inside. Sam and the sergeant jumped back as a hail of shots tore through the window. They had taken the pilot's recoilless .50: a foot-wide piece of wood was blasted from the frame.

Slowly, ignoring the bullets that crashed into the wooden planking around him, the sergeant walked out on the porch and reached down with his left hand to pick up his pistol. The rain of fire stopped as the copter rose straight up.

Carefully, in no hurry, the sergeant walked clear of the porch, flicked off the safety and raised the pistol straight-armed before him. He waited until the copter swung away and was no longer over the girl, who still lay face down in the yard, then dropped the pistol sights onto the target and pulled the trigger.

Three times the recoilless .50 boomed, coughing out its small tangent flames, and the half inch, steel-cored slugs tore chunks of aluminum from the copter's body. The whistle of the jets died and the blades slowed. Two more shots boomed out as it slanted sideways and fell into the maple grove behind the house and burst into flames. No one came out of the wreck.

"They were trying to leave the plague area," the sergeant said, as he struggled to get the gun back into his holster on his right hip with his left hand. "So it meant I had to get the copter, too." He looked unsmilingly at the dead policeman. "And Forson was a good cop." His expression changed suddenly to a mirthless smile as he tapped an enamel and gold decoration that he wore above his shield. "First place in the pistol tournament—firing with *either* hand." He started to sag and Sam caught him, led him toward the porch.

"Sit down and shut up while I put something on that hole."

Legs sprawled before him, the sergeant sat silently while Sam sprinkled sulfa on the bullet wounds, then slapped on self-adhesive bandages. Dr. Stissing came hesitantly onto the porch.

"Finish this dressing, will you, Doctor," Sam said, climbing to his feet. "I want to look at the others."

The pilot was dead, the back of his skull torn away by a rifle bullet. The tanks on the copter blew up just then with muffled thuds and no one had emerged from the crumpled cabin: the men inside were beyond his help. Sam went over to the girl, who was still lying face in the dirt and sobbing painfully.

"I'm a doctor——" he said, but when he touched her shoulder she shivered away from him and only sobbed harder. Sam wanted to move her into the house and examine her, but without using force: perhaps Stissing might be able to help.

"Doctor," he called, "do you know this girl?"

Stissing, blinking nearsightedly, came down from the porch and bent to look at the girl's face.

"Looks like the Leslie girl——" He moved her hands away from in front of her face. "Come on, Katy, stand up and let's go into the house; there's no sense in lying out here."

With the doctor's gentle urging she climbed to her feet and pulled her torn cotton dress about her, then let him help her inside. They passed the sergeant, sitting on the steps and scowling fiercely at the wreck of the copter, and went into the parlor, where Katy dropped onto the couch. Sam went to find some blankets while Stissing made an examination.

"Nothing serious, physical that is," Stissing said afterward, out of the girl's hearing. "Scratches, contusions, what you might expect in a rape and assault, I've had them before. That's not my big worry. The girl saw her father killed; he's a widower and they live alone, the other side of town. These men broke into the house, looters she said, from somewhere in Jersey, drunk and nasty, and when they started to fool around with her, her father swung on them. Killed him, right in front of her, set fire to the house, probably burnt, I never saw or heard of anything like this before, not around here . . ."

"We saw the house on the way in, leveled to the ground. Something will have to be done about these patients of yours."

"Phone's out," the sergeant said, coming out of the house. "Not the wire either, I checked that. We better be going."

"You're in no condition to go anywhere . . ."

"It'll take more than that little bullet hole to strand me up here in the woods."

"You can take my car," Stissing said, "it's in the barn. I'll stay here with Hadley and the girl until you can get some help from the county hospital. They can bring the car back."

"Sorry, Doctor," the sergeant said. "But those bowbs got to your car first. Pulled out the ignition. Only way out of here is by walking."

Sam thought about it for a moment. "You're probably right. There can't be many of these looting gangs around or we would have heard about it, so we shouldn't run into any more. You'll be safe enough here, Dr. Stissing, just keep the windows and doors locked and we'll get some help to you as soon as we have contacted the local police. Let me get my bag, Sergeant, then we can go."

"One thing first, Doctor—if you don't mind. Could you undo my belt and slip my holster around to the left side so I can get at it easier? Be a big help."

They walked in the center of the road, going back toward the town. The first house they passed had all the shades pulled down and was sealed up: no one came to the door, even when they knocked loudly. At the next farm, a red brick building set back from the road, they had a response even before they knocked—a gun barrel protruded from the partly open window on the porch.

"Just stop there," the unseen man behind the gun called out.

"I'm a police officer," the sergeant said with cold anger. "Now put that weapon away before you get into trouble."

"How do I know what you are? You got a city cop's uniform on, but I never seen you before. You could of stolen it. Move on—I don't want trouble."

"We want to use your phone, that's all," Sam said.

"Phone's out, trouble at the exchange."

"Do you have a car——"

"I got a car and it's staying right here in case I need it, now get moving! You may have the plague from space for all that I know and I'm not talking any more—move!" The gun barrel wiggled up and down.

"Strategic retreat," Sam said, taking the angry sergeant by the arm and pulling him away. "There's nothing here worth getting shot for."

"Rubes!" the sergeant grumbled.

The town of Stonebridge was sealed as tight as the farmhouses and there were no cars in sight. They continued through it and toward the highway just a mile down the road. They heard the sound at the same time, coming from somewhere ahead, and they stopped, the sergeant with his hand on his gun.

"I've done enough duck hunting to recognize that—it's a shotgun."

"Two of them—sounds like a private war."

"If you don't mind, Doctor, I'll walk in front since I've got the only weapon."

They went along the shoulder of the road, close to the trees, as silently as they could. There was another farm ahead, half seen through the trunks of the oak trees, and running figures. A woman screamed and another shot sounded. The sergeant had his gun out and a cold smile on his face as he slipped forward.

"Looks like his time we're here when the trouble is just starting . . ." He raised his gun.

There was a truck parked by the side of the road, its outline through the leaves strangely familiar to Sam. He ran forward and deflected the sergeant's gun arm.

"What are you doing? Those are looters . . ."

"I don't think so—isn't that an Army half-track over there?"

Once around the bend they could see the olive-drab truck

clearly, with the leafy branch framed globe insignia of the UN stenciled on its armored side. They passed it and turned into the farmyard where the screams had turned into a gasping sob. A burly corporal was embarrassedly holding a woman by the shoulders while she cried into the apron raised before her face. A lieutenant was supervising two soldiers who were spreading poison grain in the chicken run behind the house. Next to it was another wire enclosure with an open gate and on the ground outside the scattered bodies of a number of turkeys, while another of the birds was perched on the branch of the oak tree to which the ropes of a children's swing were tied. A soldier below the tree raised and fired a repeating shotgun and the pellets tore the bird from its perch. The shot echoed away into silence among the trees until the woman's muffled sobbing was the only sound. The officer turned around when they approached: like the other soldiers he had a New Zealand flash on his shoulder. His eyes jumped quickly from the bandaged police sergeant to Sam's white clothes and black bag.

"If you are a physician I should say your arrival is well timed. The farmwife here——" The lieutenant pointed to the woman who was still sobbing uncontrollably.

"Has she been injured?" Sam asked.

"No, not physically, but she's been hysterical, bit of a shock or whatever you call it. We've been running into this sort of trouble all along the line, these rural people take a very dim view of our killing off their stock. This woman opened the run and released those turkeys, then tried to stop my men. At least the farmer here is being reasonable, some of them have attempted to stop us with guns; he's in the house with the children."

Sam looked at the woman and while the soldier was still holding her he swabbed her shoulder and administered an intramuscular injection of Denilin, the quick-acting sedative. By the time he had led her into the house she was staggering and, with her grim-faced husband's aid, Sam put her to bed.

"She'll sleep at least twelve hours," he said. "If she is still bad when she wakes up give her one of these, one pill will keep her calmed down for twenty-four hours." He put a small bottle of psychotropic tablets by the bed.

"They killing all our chickens and turkeys, Doctor, they got no right."

"It's not a matter of right—it's a matter of necessity. Those birds carry the disease that could kill your entire

64

family. And you've been given a receipt; they'll be paid for or replaced after the emergency."

"Just a piece of paper," the farmer muttered.

Sam started to say something, then thought better of it. He went out and found the police sergeant and the Army officer in conversation, bent over a map.

"The sergeant has been telling me about your troubles," the lieutenant said. "I wish I could provide you with transportation back to the city, but I'm afraid I can't, I have only this single vehicle. But there is a compromise possible. The farms here are close together and I can take my men to the next one or two of them on foot while the driver runs you over to this spot." He pointed to the map. "Your Dewey Thruway passes right here at Southfields and there should be a number of convoys going south. You can flag down one of the lorries. Will that suit you?"

"Yes, that will be fine. One other thing, I want to send a message back to my hospital, and I'm sure the sergeant wants to contact his squad too, but the phones aren't operating. Do you have a radio in your truck?"

"We have, but it can only send and receive on the Army command channels. You can't talk directly but I could have the messages relayed for you."

"Suits me," the sergeant said, opening his notebook. He tore a sheet out and handed it to Sam, then carefully printed a message of his own with his left hand. Sam thought a moment; this would be read by a lot of people and he did not want to be too specific about the reasons for the report. He wrote:

Dr. McKay Bellevue Hospital New York City—Results negative case of common furunculosis. Bertolli

It was dusk when they reached the thruway and the UN corporal used his flashlight to signal a convoy of food trucks. A command car stopped with guns ready since there had been more than one attempted looting—and then drove them back slowly to the city. It was after nine before Sam reached the hospital and checked back in.

"There's a message for you, Doctor," the girl said, flipping rapidly through her file until she found the envelope with his name on it. He tore it open and found a single slip of paper inside with a rapid scrawl in thick marking pencil on it.

CALL ME AT ONCE EXT. 782 98 NITA

There was an air of urgency in the handwriting that struck

65

a warning note. He went to one of the booths in the hall and quickly dialed the number.

"Hello," he said when the image cleared, "I have your message . . ."

"Sam, are you alone?" she asked, and he couldn't help noticing that her eyes were wider open than normal and that there was a thin shrill to the edges of her words.

"Yes, what is it?"

"Can you come here at once? It's laboratory 1242."

"I'm on my way—but what is it about?"

"I—I can't tell you on the phone, it's too terrible!"

She broke the connection and her features swam, melted and disappeared.

8

Nita was waiting in the open door of the lab when he came out of the elevator and she let him in without saying a word, then locked the door securely behind him.

"You're being very secretive—can you tell me now what is going on?"

"I'll show you, Sam, everything that I have been doing and what the results have been, then let you decide for yourself."

"You said on the phone that there was something terrible, what did you mean?"

"Please," she asked, and Sam saw that when she clamped her lips shut they were so tight they were white. "Just look first and make your own mind up, without asking me any more questions." She pointed to the racked test tubes and specimens. "I've been doing graded tests for the team on the resistance of the Rand virus, just getting empirical results that can be fed to the computers so that they might be useful to the other researchers. This has left me with some spare time and I have been doing some tests on my own, consecutive isolation passages and repeated transfers to tissue cultures."

"There must be other teams doing this?"

"There are. I didn't mind duplicating somebody else's work since I was doing this outside of the assigned tests. I guess, what I was really hoping, was that after repeated transfers the virus might be weakened or changed and we could treat it successfully, but it stays just as deadly as ever. But I did find out something else . . ."

"What?"

"Just check the results first." Close-lipped, she handed him a folder and waited patiently while he flipped through the sheets.

"Everything looks in order, as you said—wait a moment, this is an interesting series. You were alternating tissues, first bird, then human?"

"Yes, I used the laboratory birds, pigeons, and Detroit-6 human tissue culture, first one and then the other. I made seven transfers in all and ended up with Rand-beta virus from the bird, still just as deadly as ever, only it had one factor changed, something I had not counted on and only discovered by accident. In there——"

Nita pointed to a sealed isolation cage and Sam pulled the covering cloth away and looked inside. A dog lay on its side on the floor of the cage, panting heavily. Through the thin fur covering its belly could be seen round, reddened swellings. He dropped the cover and looked back to Nita, his face drained of blood.

"You've made the tests——?" She nodded. "Then, this dog, it has Rand's disease."

"Yes, Rand-gamma I suppose we should call it, something new. None of the other strains of Rand, neither alpha nor beta will infect canines, not even after six transfers from human to bird. But here, on the seventh transfer, something new. Something incredible . . ."

"I've never heard of anything like it!" Sam was pacing the floor, angrily, burning with frustration at this last development. Rand's disease was an alien plague, inhuman—was there no way to stop it?

"Have you tried to find out susceptibility of other organisms to this Rand-gamma? Does McKay know what you have found out?"

She shook her head. "No, I've gone just this far and—then I was frightened. I left the message for you; if you weren't back soon I was going to call Dr. McKay What shall we do, Sam?"

"See McKay as soon as possible, tell him what you've done. He s not going to like it—do you realize what this will mean?"

"Yes," she said so faintly he could barely hear her. She dropped into a chair.

"If we stop the spread of the disease in birds we should have it licked—but what if we can't stop it before it turns into Rand-gamma? Then it will be the dogs, and what after that? These mutations and changes are incredible, they're like nothing we have ever heard of before—they don't follow any earthly pattern. But, is it possible there is an alien pattern they conform to? If we can find it, find its rules, then we can stop it."

"But it's not an alien disease, Sam—it's human, or earthly, whatever you want to call it."

"Now it is, but it came on the ship from Jupiter, it must be a disease from that planet———"

"No, that's been determined already." She riffled through a thick stack of duplicated reports until she found one which she handed to Sam. "You can see for yourself; this is still a preliminary report but it is indicative. They simply cannot get the virus to live under anything resembling Jupiter conditions. When the temperature drops and the pressure is raised the virus dies, long before it reaches the range of the Jupiter atmosphere."

"That's impossible!"

"Everything about this virus is impossible—but it is here. We can't escape that fact. What can we do, Sam? I feel defeated at every turn . . ."

"There's not very much we can do by ourselves—but that's what McKay's team is for. They'll find out the significance of these changes." He took her hands to help her to her feet, and was aware of how cold they were, while her face was pale under the makeup and her eyes red-rimmed with fatigue. "We'll turn all the results over to him, then you'll get some rest. When was the last time you slept?"

"I've been dozing on the couch here, it's enough———" She looked at herself in the mirror and bit her lip, then laughed, searching through her purse for a comb. "You're right—it's not enough. I look like a refugee from a horror film. Give me a moment to repair some of the ravages and then we'll go see McKay."

"I'll call and find out if he is in his office."

There was difficulty in getting Dr. McKay's number and Sam hung up and tried again. Twice after this he got busy signals before he finally got through. The call signal buzzed a number of times before the secretary answered it.

"I'm sorry, it is impossible to talk to Dr. McKay, he cannot be disturbed——" She disconnected before Sam had a chance to say a word. She was distraught and seemed to be on the point of tears.

"I wonder what the trouble can be . . ." Sam said, looking at the dark screen. "She seemed very upset about something."

"We'll have to go and find out," Nita said, putting her notes into a folder. "Though I don't wonder at her cracking a bit. The strain has been simply awful here and it doesn't show any signs of letting up."

The elevator boosted them with a silent rush to the thirty-ninth floor, but when the doors opened a murmur of voices pushed in, a chilling novelty in the normally silent hospital. They stepped out just in time to see a stretcher with a white-covered figure being wheeled into the service elevator further down the hall. A small crowd had gathered around the open door of McKay's office and Sam recognized one of the nurses who had shared the same tour with him in the emergency room: he touched her shoulder.

"What happened, Ann?"

"It's Dr. McKay." She looked worried—as well as tired, like everyone else in the giant hospital. "He's been over-working, you know—it was so sudden, a coronary thrombosis they think, he just collapsed."

Sam pushed through the crowd at the door and Nita followed him. There were fewer people inside and the secretary was gone. The door to McKay's private office was partly open and Sam could see Eddie Perkins inside, talking on the phone. He knocked quietly and Eddie glanced up and waved them in, signaling them to shut the door at the same time.

"Yes, of course," Perkins said into the phone, "we'll keep going here and I'll keep you informed of Dr. McKay's condition. Right then, good-by." He disconnected and scratched a cigarette out of the open package on the desk before him. "It's a mess, Sam. Everyone acts like it is the end of the world with McKay out of the battle; they think he is going to lick Rand's disease all by himself and the team is just sort of a Greek chorus to cheer him on." The phone whirred and he gave it a distasteful look and put his cigarette out. It was the governor of New York State and Eddie gave him three minutes of solid reassurance before pleading the rush of business and hanging up.

"Do you see what I mean?" he asked, relighting the bent cigarette.

"You can't blame them," Sam said. "After all McKay did find the answer to Topholm's pachyacria and they expect him to pull another cat out of the same bag. Who is going to take over for him?"

"Your guess is as good as mine. I've been his acting assistant the last few days, so I'm holding on to the strings until something is decided. Chabel and the team heads will be here for a meeting in an hour."

"Well, until they decide something you're top man, Eddie."

"Yes," Perkins said thoughtfully, a double stream of smoke coming slowly from his nose, "I imagine I am. In which case—what can I do for you?"

Nita opened the file and passed the sheets across the desk, outlining briefly what she had discovered. Perkins flipped through them while she talked, looking up sharply when she mentioned the dog that had been affected.

"You make it sound pretty bad, Nita." He closed the file and pushed it away from him. "In the morning I'll let one of the pathologists have a look at this, see what they think. Meantime, thanks for the homework, we'll see if we can put it to some use."

"Eddie, you don't seem to get the importance of this," Sam said, smiling to take the edge off his words. "If Rand's disease can be passed on to dogs we're in for some bad trouble. Birds as vectors are bad enough——"

"I told you I'd take care of it, Sam, now relax." There was an edge to Perkins's voice now.

"There's nothing to relax about; dogs are going to get this disease and if they are then now is the time to take measures."

"Like starting to kill all the dogs around—birds aren't bad enough? Do you know the trouble we've been running in to with that?"

"The trouble isn't important. If we have to kill the dogs we'll kill them—better now than after they've been infected."

"Dr. Bertolli, let's not forget one thing," Perkins's voice was empty of tone, his long face cold and drawn. "You are an intern in this hospital and not one who makes decisions. This will be taken care of——"

"Come off it, Eddie, when we were both students——"

"That will be *enough!*" Perkins crashed his hand down on the desk.

Sam took a long breath and let it out slowly, keeping his temper in check, then climbed to his feet. "Let's go, Nita," he said.

"Just a minute," Perkins said. He was also standing now and leaning forward on his arms, his fists planted squarely on his desk. "You don't know everything that is going on. There are two factors that you happen to be ignorant of: firstly, we have had some success today with a vaccine that may have arrested some early cases of Rand's; secondly, we are not going to allow this disease seven passages through different hosts as Dr. Mendel has done. That's a lab exercise and we're working with the real world. We're controlling the spread of the disease and wiping out the vectors. If things keep going as they are—and even if all the cases we now have die—we'll still lick it by wiping out the reservoirs of infection. So don't rock the boat."

"Is that all, Dr. Perkins?" Sam asked, no sign of his anger showing.

"That's all. You stick to your job and I'll stick to mine." The phone whirred and he sat down to answer it. They left.

They said nothing until they had gone down the hall and were waiting for the elevator. Nita looked worriedly at his tightly clenched jaw and could feel the knotted muscles in the forearm when she touched it.

"Sam—please, don't let it bother you so. The others will see . . ."

"The others will see nothing if he doesn't show the report to them! He's playing politics again, don't you realize that? Don't rock the damned boat—what a wonderful way to practice medicine!"

"Yet he's right in a way, as long as things are going smoothly outside and they're bringing the cases under control . . ."

"But they're not going smoothly, I've seen enough of what's going on to realize that. And that's not the point. Smooth or not, we must take the right measures or this plague will spread to every corner of the world."

As the elevator doors opened before them its loudspeaker

broke into life and was echoed by the other speakers in the hall behind them.

"Dr. Roussell, Dr. Christensen, Dr. Bertolli, Dr. Invar. Will you please report to the Emergency Room. Dr. Roussell, Dr. Christensen . . ."

"What can it be?" Nita asked, looking at him with worried eyes.

"More trouble. The boat is being rocked in spite of Dr. Edward Perkins. Look, Nita, don't wait for him to make up his mind—send a copy of your findings to Professor Chabel at World Health."

"I couldn't, that would be going over his head!"

"Try not to be so sweet and civilized, that's a luxury we are going to have to forego for a while. Let Chabel know." He stepped inside the elevator as the doors closed, then was gone from her sight.

"Sam Bertolli, I just don't know what to make of you," she said to herself as she rang for the next elevator. It was a civilized world and a well-ordered world, and he just didn't seem to fit into it at times. When the elevator arrived she saw that there were stains on the smooth white walls and drops of fresh blood on the gray floor. She shivered. Perhaps the world was not as ordered and civilized as she supposed.

"Another riot, that's all I know," Roussell said. "Move your big dirty feet, Chris—this is my last pair of whites." Dr. Christensen, who was sprawled on his back occupying most of the room on the stretcher, only rattled a guttural snore in answer. The other three interns looked at him enviously, rocking back and forth as the ambulance raced through the deserted streets. They had all been on continuous duty longer than they cared to remember.

"What's the city like now?" Sam asked. "I've been out in the woods all day running down a supposed cure for Rand's disease."

"No cure?" Invar asked.

"No disease. Boils. The doctor was old, enthusiastic, near-sighted and should have been put out to pasture thirty years ago."

"The city's falling apart," Roussell said. "People think we're lying when we tell them they can't catch Rand's from each other but only from birds. So everything is closed up tight. Rioting, violence, break-ins, rape, religious nuts, drunks.

72

It's just lovely. Anyone have a benny? It looks like another night without sleep."

"It's fear," Invar said. "People are afraid to leave their homes so the normal city life has broken down. The military is keeping most of the essential services like electricity and phones going, and they have been trucking in food, but they can't keep it up forever—not in a city this size. Tension is building and there has been a constant run of new cases of the plague—people can see that and their nerves are getting rubbed raw—and the ban on all traveling is the last straw. It makes good epidemiological sense but to the guy in the street it looks like he is going to be trapped on this rock until he dies."

"He may be right," Sam said, thinking of Nita's experiment with the dog.

"No depressing thoughts, Doctor!" Roussell said, raising his eyebrows. "We must be brave, clean, reverent——"

"That's for boy scouts, not physicians. Neither rain nor hail nor gloom of night——"

"And that's for postmen," Christensen mumbled, rolling over on the stretcher. "Now will you bunch of old women kindly shut up so I can get some sleep."

A police car passed them with a wail of its siren and in the distance they heard the hurried clanging of a fire engine. In the background, growing louder and more ominous, a roar like distant breakers.

"What the hell?"

"A mob, Doctor, the citizens of our fair state showing their resentment of constituted authority."

"They sound like animals."

"They are," Christensen said, opening his eyes and groaning. "We all are. Just below the surface the red-eyed beast lurks. So into battle, Doctors. What was it old Shakespeare said? 'Once more unto the breach, dear friends!'"

The ambulance lurched to a stop and when Sam threw the rear door open the harsh roar of a multitude of voices poured in. The bantering, the moment of good-natured attempt to forget the world outside was ended. As their expressions changed, firmed, they were physicians again. They climbed down as the driver hurried around to help them unload the stretchers.

It was a nightmare scene. The ambulance had stopped under one of the soaring arches of an approach to the Wagner Bridge on Twenty-third Street. It rose above them, its three

73

wide levels brightly lit but empty of traffic, stretching out across the Hudson River to New Jersey. Around the maze of entrances and exits a dark crowd had gathered, screaming with a single voice of hatred, their faces blue-lit by the mercury vapor lamps or ruddy from the torches they carried. Behind them a row of old warehouses was burning. Shots snapped over their heads from the beleaguered forces of police and Army and were drowned in the roaring splash of the fire hoses. Knots of uniformed defenders could be picked out by the glare of the battle lamps they had put behind the barriers of trucks and metal drums thrown across the roadway. This was the setting, the shifting backdrop to the emergency dressing station that had been set up here, boldly lit by the piercing light of the battle lamps. In harsh black and white the huddled bodies of the injured lay waiting for treatment; behind them were those to whom treatment would never come, the newly dead.

"Doctor, can you help me— Doctor!"

Sam heard the words clearly through the thunder of background noise and turned to see a young medical corpsman waving to him: he shouldered the emergency bag and threaded his way toward him through the sprawled figures.

"They just brought her over, Doctor, I don't know what to do——"

The corpsman was young, hardly out of his teens, and he had never seen anything like this before. He had practiced in training and he had probably treated gunshot and puncture wounds—but never a woman who had one leg and her entire side burned, crisped black, with clothing and flesh charred together. His pressure can of burn foam had run out before he had done her leg as high as her knee and he just looked at it with staring eyes, pressing the useless button.

"I'll attend to this," Sam said, noticing the woman's fixed expression and gaping mouth. "Take care of that policeman there, pressure bandage for the bullet wound." As the corpsman turned away Sam pressed his telltale to the woman's arm, knowing the results in advance. Massive fourth-degree burns, shock, then death. He pulled a blanket over her and turned to the next case.

Lacerations, gunshot wounds, broken bones, fractured skulls. Most of the injured were soldiers or policemen, the few civilians were those who had been trampled or crushed in the attack. The rioters were using any weapons they could lay their hands on in their hysterical attempts to flee the city.

Sam finished securing a dressing on a policeman's arm, then sent him to the ambulance, and when he turned back he noticed a new arrival leaning against one of the pillars with both hands over his face. He was in the shadows and when Sam pulled him gently forward into the light he saw that the soldier was wearing a turban on his head and had the chevrons of a havildar; one of the Pakistani brigade that had been flown in early that morning. His hands were. clamped to cover his face but blood was oozing out from between his fingers and dripping steadily to the ground.

"Over here," Sam said, guiding him to an empty stretcher and helping him to lie down. "If you'll move your hands away, Havildar, I'll take care of that."

The soldier opened the one eye that was not covered by his hands. "I dare not, Doctor," he said in a strained voice. "If I do my face shall fall away."

"You just let me worry about that, it's my job." Sam pushed at the man's hands gently and they reluctantly moved back. Fresh blood welled up and he could see the curving, almost circular laceration that cut through the cheek to the bone and had torn one nostril away from his nose: broken bits of glass still stuck in the flesh.

"A broken bottle?" Sam asked, making an injection with a morphine syrette.

"Yes, Doctor, he came on me suddenly and pushed it into my face before I could stop him. Then I—I'm afraid, contrary to orders—I hit him full in the stomach with the butt of my rifle, he fell down and I came here."

"I would have done the same myself."

Sam took the last of the visible glass out with tweezers—if there was more they would find it in the hospital—and set the width and depth of the stitch on the battery operated suturator. Holding the edges of the wound together with the fingers of his left hand he pressed the tiny machine over the cut. Each time it touched it secured the cut edges with a rapid suture—sewn together, tied and cut free in a fraction of a second. He moved it on, making a few large stitches that would secure the wound until the surgeons could attend to it. No large blood vessels had been cut and the bleeding had almost stopped.

When the Pakistani had been dispatched by ambulance

with the other cases needing immediate attention Sam found two soldiers waiting for him. The sergeant saluted.

"We have some wounded up there on the top deck, Doctor —can you help us?"

"How many—and what is the situation?"

"Just two—now, a pair of the men hit by thrown metal, but we are expecting more trouble. We've set up a second blockade there because we haven't enough men to hold all the entrances. The others will be falling back on it soon and then you'll have your work cut out for you."

Sam didn't hesitate; swinging his bag onto his shoulder he pointed to two emergency medical boxes that had been unloaded from the ambulance.

"Let's go then, and bring those with you."

A big, double-vaned combat copter was waiting for them, jets whistling softly. Once they were in, it lifted straight up with an ear-shattering howl, swung over the top deck of the bridge and dropped gently behind a barrier of overturned trucks and cars. Nervous-looking soldiers manned the barricade—the mob couldn't be seen from here but its raw sound beat on the air. Sam watched the boxes being unloaded, then turned his attention to the two casualties. One man had a brain concussion and would probably lose his eye, the other had a lacerated wound that a field dressing took care of. There were shouts close by as the soldiers attached thick fire hoses to the standpipes on either side of the bridge and unrolled them up to the barrier. Running footsteps splatted on the concrete from the other side of the barricade and more soldiers, many with torn uniforms and bandages, began climbing over.

"Get ready!" a captain shouted. "They're through the first barricades. Into the line you men, stand ready with the mortars."

Sam stood up on the fender of the command car, behind the officer, and had a clear view down the wide expanse of roadway. It was empty, outside of the scattered handful of soldiers running toward them, but they were followed by a swelling, victorious roar. This grew and grew like the cry of a great animal and then, suddenly, the road was no longer empty. From the ramps they came, and up the stairways, a solid, black, frightening mass of humanity, a mob without leadership or plans but driven on by fear and the need to survive. They came swiftly, the first rank already visible as individuals waving clubbed lengths of metal and wood; their mouths gaped open redly but whatever they were shouting was lost in the roar of the masses behind them.

A whistle shrilled behind Sam and was followed instantly by the smacking thud of the mortars: they were zeroed in nicely and the shells fell in a neat row across the width of the roadway exploding outward with gray arms of gas. The crowd shivered to a stop before it came to the expanding clouds and its voice rose in a frustrated howl.

"Will the gas stop them?" Sam asked.

"It hasn't before," the captain said tiredly.

More of the gas shells were popping into the growing haze, but a strong breeze down the river rolled the cloud away. Some people were already coming through it, staggering and falling and holding their streaming eyes. Then there were others, more and more, and the mob was upon them.

"Hoses!" a hoarse voice shouted and columns of solid water leaped out, sweeping the legs from under the rioters, bowling them over and over. Again the wordless howl rose up as they retreated from the barlike streams of water.

"Look out!" Sam shouted, but he couldn't be heard five feet away in the din.

A man had climbed up one of the supports from the lower level and was hauling himself over the balustrade. He had a large kitchen knife clamped in his teeth, pirate style, and it had cut the corner of his mouth so that the blood trickled down his chin. One of the soldiers saw him and turned toward him as the rioter grabbed the knife and leaped down; they fell together. The attacker rose, the knife now darkened with blood, but before he could move the nearest soldier had caught him on the side of the neck with the flat edge of his hand, a wicked judo blow, hitting him again on the same spot as he was falling, then kicking the knife away. The attacker was groaning, rolling over and over clutching his throat, when Sam ran up, while the soldier who had been knifed was climbing unsteadily to his knees, looking mystifiedly at his blood-drenched arm.

"Sit down," Sam said, easing him back to the roadway, then cutting his shirt open. There was a deep gash in the upper arm, more painful than serious, and Sam bound it with an antiseptic pressure bandage. The roar of the mob still beat in his ears and it seemed to have changed tone; was it more excited, with a note of elation? And behind it, low-pitched but throbbing louder was a new sound. And through it cut the shrill of a whistle. Sam looked up to see the captain waving wildly from the command car, urging on the noncoms who were pulling the soldiers from the barricade. Then he jumped down too and ran toward the outer rail near Sam as the throbbing rumble grew to a vibrating roar.

The large trailer truck must have been doing sixty miles an hour when it hit the barrier, knocking it aside. One of the front tires blew and it began to skid sideways across the roadway, the black bulk of the trailer folding up on the cab of the tractor while all sixteen wheels squealed in agony, brakes locked tight, dragged along and spewing pieces of burned rubber. It crashed into the guardrail on the far side of the road and shuddered to a stop, the cab tilted forward and one wheel hanging into space.

That was all that Sam saw before the mob burst through the gap, unstoppable and victorious. They ignored the soldiers, even the remains of the two who had been caught and crushed like ants by the plunging truck, and rushed headlong down the bridge. Fear drove them on and ahead was freedom.

"They will never get through," the captain said, his lips pulled back from his teeth in a pained expression. "The New Jersey police have barricaded and blocked the other end of this bridge solidly and are waiting for them. They killed my men—I wish they *could* get through!"

"What do you mean?" Sam asked.

"I mean that we have no orders to shoot or defend ourselves, as do the New Jersey police. But there is a ring further away, I don't know how far out, and they are determined to keep this plague inside of it. They have bulldozed buildings and plowed this ring clear and are putting up barbed wire all along it." He looked away from his dead men and mastered his anger with a tremulous sigh, and when he spoke again it was with a weary sadness. "And they have orders, I saw them . . . that anyone who enters the ring and attempts to cross the wire is to be shot."

There was little sound from the mob now, other than the trample of running feet, as they surged through the opening in the barricade. It was a mile to the other end of the bridge and they needed their breath. Above the thud of their foot-steps sounded the whistling flutter of a copter and when Sam looked up he could see the riding lights coming toward them down the river. The pilot must have seen the military copter behind the barricade because he swung out in a circle and began to descend, lifting once when the people streamed by below, then dropping again when the flow lessened and

78

moved away. When the copter entered the glow of the bridge lights Sam saw that it had the Connecticut State Trooper's insignia on its side.

Rioters were still coming in the gap, though not in the solid mass as at first. The captain pushed his way angrily through them and Sam followed: there would be injuries on the other side of the barricade. As they passed the copter, its blades still swinging slowly, the pilot slid his window open and called down to them.

"Listen, I'm just down from Waterbury and I don't know this town—can you help me?"

"I'm from Karachi and I know less about it than you do," the captain said, moving on by.

"Where do you want to go?" Sam asked, glancing around at the same time to see if there were any casualties.

"Bellevue Hospital—do you know where it is?"

"Yes, that's my hospital. What is it you want there?" For no reason at all Sam had a premonition, a chilling sensation that brushed the length of his spine.

"Delivery to make; can you show me the way to their heliport? I got a dog in the back, a dead dog, all wrapped up in plastic."

The chill was a cold hand now that clutched at Sam as he threw back the piece of canvas that covered the dog and turned his flashlight down on its body, dimly seen through the many layers of sealed polythene.

But it was not so well concealed that he couldn't see the raw, ugly, red boils that covered its skin.

9

Darkness filled the laboratory, pierced only by the blue-green light from the TV screen that glowed above the workbench, throwing its ghostly illumination over Sam's face and accenting even more the lines of fatigue and the dark shadows under his eyes. He looked at the image on the screen and hated it. The jumbled and fearfully twisted rods of Rand's virus sprawled across the face of the tube, transmitted from the main virology lab, glowing in room after room of the great hospital like some duplicated and demonic icon. Sam yawned and forced his eyes away from it: he should sleep, he was tired enough surely, but sleep would not come. Outside the window a grayness was beginning to seep through the rain that had been falling most of the night. He should have slept. Nita had leaned her head forward onto her arm while they had been talking and just that easily and quickly had been asleep, the wealth of her hair spread out on the table. She breathed lightly, her half-turned face lovely in its composure.

An announcing signal pinged and the scene on the screen shifted and changed, yet did not change. The latticework of thin rods still stretched from edge to edge: the speaker hummed.

"Identification is positive, the furuncles of the specimen, the dog, sent in from Connecticut, contain the virus of Rand's disease, it's on the screen now. Until further tests have been run on the viability of this virus in other mediums and hosts we are tentatively assigning it the title of Rand-gamma . . ."

Nita sat back in her chair, straightening her hair while she listened intently to the voice, blinking a bit with her sleep-filled eyes at the image on the screen.

"It came too fast," Sam said, his fists clenched in impotent anger. "There should have been more time before the change took place, before the disease passed through seven different hosts. It's been less than a week now."

"Yet it is happening, we can't escape the fact——"

"There are a lot of facts we can't escape, right out there in the city." Sam was on his feet, pacing the length of the room, tired but too angry to sit still. "The entire plague area is falling apart, sliding back to savagery; I've been watching it happen. I've never realized before what a thin veneer civilization is—it has taken us centuries to develop but only days to lose."

"Aren't you being unfair, Sam? People are just afraid."

"Of course I know they're afraid, I'm afraid myself and I have more to fear because I know just how easily Rand's disease is spread and how helpless we are against it. But I also know what they seem to have forgotten, that not our strongest but *only* hope is our brains, our ability to think before acting. Yet out there people are acting without thinking and in doing it they are condemning themselves to certain death and trying to drag the rest of the world down with them. They riot and they get killed. They ignore the sound advice given to them and shelter their miserable chickens and parakeets. Wait until we try and kill their dogs! Not my old Rex, my dear old friend!—when Rex is really the damned enemy now who is going to catch a disease that will kill him and his idiot master. But before they die they are going to panic. I've been watching it and it's a disgusting sight because there are no people in a mob, just animals. I've watched them rape and kill and try to get away and eventually someone will escape, we won't be able to stop it. Someone will break out of the quarantine zone, or an infected dog will get through and the disease will keep spreading. People!"

Her voice was as quiet as his had been booming.

"You can't blame people for having emotions, Sam—it's only human——"

"I'm as human as the next man," he said, stopping in front of her, "and I have just as many emotions. I know how those people out there feel, because I hear the same little lost simian screaming in my own heart. But what do we have intelligence for if we can't use it to control or guide the emotions?"

"Just like a man to talk about guiding emotions while you're stamping up and down the floor in a rage."

He opened his mouth to answer, then stopped and smiled instead.

"You're right of course. All my raging isn't going to accomplish a thing. It's the times I suppose, with all our emotions laid bare and exposed like a raw nerve. The next thing you know I'll be telling you how lovely you look sitting there in the blue light of Rand's virus with your hair all in a tangle."

"Does it look awful?" she asked worriedly, trying to pat it back into position.

"No, leave it," he said and reached out to take her hand away. When his skin touched hers something changed and she glanced up at him quickly and he saw a reflection of what he was feeling mirrored in her eyes. When he pulled at her hand to draw her to her feet he found that she was already rising.

When he lowered his face he found her lips waiting.

A kiss is a contact, a union, an exchange. It is unknown to

certain races and tribes, while others know it and consider it with disgust. They all suffer a loss. A kiss can be a cold formula, or a token of familial relationship or a prelude to the act of love. It can also be a revelation in an unspoken, secret language of feelings that have never been expressed in words.

She lowered her face against his chest afterward and he knew that she was smiling while he spoke because he traced the contours of her lips with his fingers.

"I suppose—all our emotions are closer to the surface now and we say and do things just as we feel them. I have to laugh at myself——"

"Please don't, Sam!"

"—Well, I should laugh at myself. If you only knew how I loathe starry-eyed and out of focus TV love scenes of young things wallowing in the treacly embrace of love at first sight. I think they have demeaned something uncountably precious by using it for common coinage. I want to be able to say that I love you, Nita, and have you understand it is something vitally different and important."

"But I love you too, so I know exactly how you feel. I suppose it is terrible to say, but I'm almost grateful for Rand's disease and what has happened. Women are selfish, darling. I have the feeling that without the pressure you would just have gone on being one of those silent, busy men, who use their lives up on important things and never have a moment to consider the frivolous unimportance of women."

"Unimportance!" Her body was alive and vital under his hands.

The phone cut a clear signal through the darkness of the room.

"Damn!" he said angrily, and Nita laughed as she pulled gently away from him.

"I know how you feel," she said, "but I still must answer it."

He smiled back and reluctantly let go as she turned on the lights and went to the phone. The rain had let up a bit, but occasional gusts of wind sent it thrumming against the window as he looked out at the moist grayness of the city, seemingly empty of all life. From the twelfth floor here he could see far up First Avenue and the only thing moving was a green and white police car: it slipped into a side street and vanished. There was a mumble of voices behind him, cut off as Nita hung up. When he turned back she was standing and stretching, an enjoyable sight that cheered him a good deal.

"I'm going to wash up and change and find some breakfast," she said. "There's going to be a meeting in an hour, probably another of those council of war things, even Professor Chabel will be there she said."

"She?"

"Dr. McKay's secretary, though I guess she's Perkins's now."

"Did she mention me? Locator knows I'm here."

"No, she just asked me to come—but of course you're supposed to be there."

"Am I? Just another intern—isn't that what Eddie Perkins called me?—at a policy meeting."

"But you must be there, Sam!"

He smiled, a little crookedly. "Oh, I'll be there all right."

It was one of the large meeting rooms, more than ample to hold the people assembled there, roughly thirty in all. Sam recognized most of them, heads of departments, researchers who had been drafted to work on the team, even two uniformed officers of the Public Health Service. Coming through the door, he had a sudden feeling of inadequacy at his presumption in coming here, but Nita must have sensed this because she pressed his hand firmly in hers as he helped her into a chair and this kept his mind off the proceedings until he was securely seated. Then it was too late to retreat, nor was it necessary. The people who knew him and happened to catch his eye just nodded or lifted a hand in greeting, while the others took no notice of him at all.

"You are Dr. Bertolli?" a rumbling, accented voice asked from behind him, and he rose quickly. The scowling man with the full, black beard and broken nose was familiar to Sam, though he had never met him.

"Yes, I am, Dr. Hattyár, what can I . . ."

"How do you feel?" Hattyár leaned forward until his face was only a few inches from Sam's. In someone else it might have been annoying, but Sam had heard the hospital stories about the Hungarian immunologist; it was generally agreed that he was a genius—his radioactive differentiator had already replaced Ouchterlony's gel precipitation in laboratory procedure—but he was known almost as well for his severe myopia and vanity. He needed corrective lenses badly but refused to admit it or to wear them. His nearsightedness was only a minor handicap in the laboratory, but it did tend to make his social life difficult. "How do you feel?" he repeated, looking at Sam closely.

"Just fatigued, Doctor, I've missed a lot of sleep—but nothing else. No symptoms at all of Rand's disease."

"Not so good, a small fever would have helped. You are sure there was no small fever——?"

"None, I'm afraid."

"Still, there is some hope. I want some of your serum. I have sera, too much of it, but always from someone who later has died. Perhaps with yours we can isolate antigens . . ."

"Sam—I thought you were on ambulance duty?" The interrupting words were matter of fact and cold, but Sam was aware of the enmity behind them. It was Eddie Perkins. He kept his own voice just as noncommittal as he turned.

"Yes, still on ambulance. I was out almost twenty hours last tour. Things aren't any better in the city."

"I see. Yes. Were you asked here?" They faced each other and the only sign of Perkins's real feelings was the cold anger in his eyes.

"No," Sam said, and caught the fleeting edge of a grin of victory.

"Well, then I'm sorry then, Sam, I'm afraid you'll have to——"

"Who the devils are you?" Hattyár boomed, leaning closer and scowling in concentration as he tried to make out the intruder's face.

"I'm Perkins, Dr. Hattyár, Dr. McKay's assistant, I'm taking over for him until . . ."

"Then go take over please, we are busy."

Hattyár wrapped his large hand around Sam's arm and pulled him away from the suddenly red-faced Perkins. Sam felt a fleeting emotion of victory, replaced instantly by the knowledge that this would only magnify his trouble with Perkins.

Professor Chabel tapped with the gavel and standing groups broke up and found seats around the long table. He sat and stared at the papers before him, squaring them into a neat stack, before he spoke in a voice heavy with the weariness they all felt.

"Firstly, I wish you all to know that this is a World Health meeting. I asked Dr. Perkins, who is seconding for Dr. McKay at the moment, to call you all together to give me an up-to-the-moment briefing. I have been receiving your reports and I must thank you all for keeping me so well informed and up to date. At World Health we have been occupied mostly with controlling the disease vectors and establishing a quarantine area and have left treatment up to local hospital authorities aided by some Army teams. But we're reaching the point where we have some major policy decisions to make, and before we do that we want to know exactly where we stand, what you are doing and what you hope to do to control this disease, everything."

When he finished speaking the entire room was silent. Finally Eddie Perkins cleared his throat and looked around. "Perhaps it might be best if I sum up the present state of our knowledge. Untreated, Rand's disease brings on death after infection in a period of roughly ten to twelve hours, in one hundred percent of the cases. To our knowledge no exceptions have been uncovered so far. However with supportive treatment we can extend that period to almost forty-eight hours. This is hopeful . . ."

"It is not hopeful, it is nothing." Dr. Hattyár's angry rumble interrupted. "It is no cure or treatment, just stretching out the time of dying."

Perkins controlled his temper with an effort. "That may be true, Dr. Hattyár, but I am just summing up roughly. Perhaps this might be a good time for you to inform us about the progress of your immunology team."

"Results zero."

"That doesn't tell us very much."

"There is nothing much to tell. Until I can isolate an antibody I can do nothing. Rand's disease is very simple, alpha, beta, gamma, all of them simple in the reactions. The organism either is infected or not. If it is infected it dies. There are no mild forms of the disease and apparently none of the organisms affected is capable of doing anything to combat the antigens. They just die."

"Could you tell me, Doctor," Chabel asked, "what you think your chances are, or rather what your prospects are of finding the antibody you need?"

"Zero. Unless a wholly new factor is introduced there is nothing that can be done."

This time the silence was even more prolonged, and a general request for further reports brought no response; Perkins had to call on the team heads by name. Many of them were not as frank as Hattyár—or could not bring themselves to be so—but their words added up to the same conclusion.

"If I may be allowed to sum up," Professor Chabel said, and there was a thin quaver to his voice that was caused by more than fatigue now, "we are not in a very good position. We know where Rand's disease came from, we know how it is spread. We know the first symptoms and we know the final result—which we can only postpone by a few hours at most. We know that none of the infected organisms can generate antibodies to combat it, antibiotics do not stop it, interferon has only a limited effect, and we have no chemical agents capable of destroying it during the course of the disease without fatally injuring the host as well. We also know, and this fact is the most unusual of all, that Rand's disease can infect certain animals, which in turn can infect their own species or reinfect humans. This is a terrible list of factors, a damning indictment, and about the only thing in our favor is that we can't infect one another."

"We can't—yet . . ." Nita said, then raised her hand toward her mouth as though regretting that she had spoken aloud. Her words were clearly audible in the quiet room and chairs squeaked as everyone turned to look toward her.

"Would you explain that, Dr. Mendel?" Chabel asked frowning.

"I'm sorry, I didn't mean to interrupt—and I have no way of proving it. Call it an unjustified assumption if you want to, but it occurred to me when I had passed Rand-beta through seven hosts and found out that it then became Rand-gamma and could infect canines——"

"Pardon me," Professor Chabel said, leafing quickly through the papers before him, "but I find no record of these experiments."

"They were not official experiments, Professor, not part of any of the planned research; I undertook them on my own and am writing up my notes now."

"Unofficial or not—you should have reported this at once, when you obtained your results!"

"I did want to——" she looked up, then glanced away quickly from Eddie Perkins, who was leaning forward, his face white and set, "—but it was just last night. When I went to see Dr. McKay he had just been stricken and there was a great deal of confusion. Soon after this the infected dog was discovered in Connecticut and the danger known."

"Confusion or not, there should have been a report. Excuse me, Doctor, I'm not criticizing you, I realize that the situation is confused as well as you do. I just wish to stress again that *anything* that has a bearing on Rand's disease—no matter how trivial it may seem—must be reported to me at once. Now please continue. You seem to feel that eventually Rand's disease will become contagious in humans?"

"I'm afraid I can't back the idea up with any facts, Professor. The disease is alien, we all admit that, and we can see that it conforms to alien laws of some kind, a growing or a changing brought on by passing through various hosts, from man to bird then to man, back and forth until suddenly it gains the capacity to infect dogs. And after passing from dog to man a number of times—then what? I have a feeling that there will be another change; it is not altogether impossible considering what has gone before, perhaps to another species of host. Or perhaps the final mutation to full contagiousness, that would seem only normal—what is abnormal is the present arrangement of inability for one human host to infect another."

"It could happen," Chabel said, nodding agreement. "Though I pray it doesn't. But whether it does or not we must be aware of the danger and I suggest a program of research into the possibility be instituted at once. Dr. Perkins, what arrangements do you suggest?"

There was a hum of cross talk as the required work was apportioned to various teams. Speaking softly, Sam leaned toward Nita and asked, "Why did you take Perkins off the hook?"

"I had to, Sam. With McKay out he's doing two men's work and we can't hang him for one mistake. You can't rock the boat."

"Don't rock the boat—that was what Perkins said—and I'd like to tip it right over. He made a bad mistake in not taking your report to Chabel and it should be mentioned and he should be canned. This is no time for mistakes."

"Aren't you being personally vindictive?"

"No, I'm not! Though I admit I would enjoy seeing it happen—no, it's more than that. He's the wrong man for the job, he proved that, and as long as he is acting for McKay we are going to have trouble . . ."

The rapping of the gavel interrupted him. Professor Chabel spoke.

"Thank you for your reports. Now I would like to tell you my reasons for asking for them. The Emergency Council of the UN has been in continuous session, with the American chiefs of staff and the President as you know, and a decision has been reached. Within a few hours we are going to begin what the Army has given the dramatic title of Operation Cleansweep, a concerted effort to halt the spread of Rand's disease at once. Zone Red, this is roughly the circular area within which the disease is now confined, will be evacuated completely. We are already beginning to move the inhabitants into a series of quarantine camps. As soon as all the developing cases of Rand's disease have appeared and have been separated, and the incubation period has been exceeded, these people will be lifted out of Zone Red. We are already widening Zone Blue, which is a strip of no-man's-land that circles Zone Red, a dead zone. We are bulldozing and leveling it, using explosives and flamethrowers where necessary, and spreading poison bait through it. Zone Blue is now about two hundred yards wide on the average and when it is done we hope it will be at least a half a mile. If nothing happens to upset our schedule we should have Zone Blue completed at the same time Zone Red is completely evacuated.

"Then Zone Red will be sown by air with radioactives having a half-life of two months."

A stunned silence followed his words as they tried to understand the magnitude of it. Over eight thousand square miles of the most metropolitan area in the world would be dead and depopulated. New York City, Newark, Philadelphia, ghost cities from which man had fled and where every bird, insect and animal down to the microscopic life in the soil would be dead. Chabel's voice continued tonelessly and grimly.

"This will have to be done at once, because the world is afraid. As long as the disease is localized and only vectored by animals Operation Cleansweep will continue." His voice dropped, so low that it could be barely heard. "This program, you must realize, is really a compromise. The people of the world are living in fear and they have a right to be. The only alternative acceptable was to drop a hydrogen bomb on Zone Red at once . . ."

He could not go on in the face of horrified expressions before him; he lowered his head, an old man who had been forced to be the mouthpiece of other people's terror—and threats.

"Dr. Chabel," Sam said, standing, a little surprised at his own temerity but being pushed ahead by the burning need to say what must be said. "Operation Cleansweep is a logical

88

answer to this problem since it can't be solved medically, at least not at once, we have all admitted that. And on a global scale it may be logical to say that an H-bomb should be dropped here—though as one of the prospective carbonized corpses I can't think very highly of the suggestion. Nor do I think very highly of the veiled threat here, that the rockets are waiting to deliver that bomb at any time it is decided that it is the best course. But that is an unimportant detail—what is more important is the unspoken desperation behind this decision—there is no medical answer, so let us scour the land clean of the infection. All very good, but there is one more piece of medical research that should be undertaken before these desperate measures are resorted to."

He stopped for breath and realized that they were all listening with an agonized intensity. They were beyond their depth in a problem that was no longer a medical one—but a matter of survival.

"What research do you talk about?" Hattyár asked impatiently.

"The spaceship 'Pericles' must be entered and searched for evidence about this disease, some records or notes. There must be a reason why Commander Rand wrote 'in ship'; after all he had survived the trip from Jupiter. If these heroic atomic measures are going to be used there can be no complaint that we will loose another plague on the earth . . ."

He was interrupted by the sharp rapping of Professor Chabel's gavel.

"Dr. Bertolli, there is nothing we can do about the 'Pericles.' Part of the decision reached by the Emergency Council was that the ship must be left untouched. The final stage of Operation Cleansweep, after evacuation and radioactive neutralizing of the land, will be the destruction of the 'Pericles' by a tactical atomic weapon. No chances are to be taken that Rand's disease, or any other plague from space, will depopulate the Earth. I'm sorry. The decision has been reached and discussion would be useless since there is no appeal; no one would listen to anything I or any of you might say. It is out of our hands. The only thing that might affect this decision would be the discovery of a treatment for Rand's disease. If that happens Operation Cleansweep might be revoked. Without a cure we are helpless to change the planned course of events."

There was little else to say. There were some protests—including a fiery one by Dr. Hattyár—but they were only for the record because they knew the decisions had already been made without their being consulted and at a far higher level. Professor Chabel listened to them all very carefully and where he could answer he did and, as soon as it was possible, he adjourned the meeting. There were no protests. Nita and Sam walked back to her laboratory together, the silence between them a tangible presence. They passed the glass doors of one of the wards, crowded with cases of Rand's disease: Nita looked away.

"I'm frightened, Sam, everything seems to be somehow . . . out of hand. This talk of bombs and radioactivity, and practically abandoning the research program. It means that these patients, and everyone else who comes down with the plague, are good as dead."

"They are dead. This decision turns us into graveyard keepers—not doctors. But look at it from the outside, from the point of view of the rest of the world. They're scared and they are going to make a sacrifice here to save themselves; let a tiny fraction of the global population die to save the rest. It makes good sense—unless you happen to be one of the fraction. It's not that decision I'm arguing with, it's the nonsensical act of sealing up the 'Pericles,' keeping it off bounds. That is an act of fear, nothing else. The answer to this plague may be in the ship, and if it is all of those already stricken may be saved."

"There's nothing we can do about it, darling, you heard what Chabel said. The ship can't be entered so we'll have to find the answer right here in the labs."

There was no one near, so she held his hand and gave it what was meant to be a touch of reassurance, then quickly took hers away. She did not notice the sudden widening of his eyes.

"Are you on duty now, Sam?" she asked as she opened the laboratory door.

"I go on in about an hour," he said, his voice steady as he went to the cabinet of instruments.

"We can't let it worry us, just go on doing—— What is that for?" She was looking at the telltale in his hand.

"Probably just foolishness, my skin temperature is probably depressed from lack of sleep, that must be why your hand felt warm to me——" He touched the telltale to her skin and the needle on the thermometer instantly wavered up to one hundred and two.

"You might be coming down with the flu, anything," he said, but he could not keep the tension from his voice.

Though there was no cure for Rand's disease, tests for its presence had been developed that were both simple and rapid.

Five minutes later they knew that the plague from space had one more victim.

10

A sick doctor is just one more patient, no different from any other and with no special privileges. The best that Sam could do was to see that Nita was put into a semiprivate room in which one bed had just been vacated; no need to ask what had happened to the last patient. He gave her the injections himself, including a heavy sedative, and when he left she was sleeping. The door closed silently and automatically behind him and he knew she was doomed, just as dead as if she had been shot with a bullet. There was no cure for Rand's disease —what could be done?

Just one thing.

There was a phone at the nurses' station and he dialed locator and told them to trace Professor Chabel, and if he hadn't left the hospital to connect them. The screen stayed dark, with just the expanding circles of the hold signal in the center, and he looked over the floor nurse's shoulder at the ward display screens. The patients were sleeping and the wards were dark but clearly revealed to the watching nurse by the infrared illumination and infrared-sensitive TV pickups. There was still no answer to his phone call. Reaching over, he dialed the number of Nita's bed on the close-up screen, and her face appeared over the current readings from the telltales. She was weakening . . .

"I have Professor Chabel, Doctor."

He cleared the close-up screen and turned to the phone.

"Professor Chabel, I would like to see you; it's urgent."

"I was just leaving the hospital . . ."

"This can be done very quickly, just a moment if you don't mind."

Chabel peered out from the tiny screen, as though trying to define Sam's thoughts. Then, "If you insist, but you had better come at once. I'm in 3911."

On the way down in the elevator he remembered that this was McKay's office, which meant that Eddie Perkins would be there too. It couldn't be helped, the matter was too urgent. The secretary showed him in at once; Chabel was behind the desk packing papers into his briefcase and Perkins was at the window, drawing heavily on a cigarette.

"What do you want?" Chabel asked, without preamble, and strangely curt.

"I want to go into the ship, the 'Pericles.' The ship must be investigated . . ."

"Impossible, you know that, you heard the decision."

"Damn the decision! We're here and it's our problem, and we can't be dictated to by a meeting in Stockholm. They are worried only about the possible danger, but we can arrange it so that there is no danger. I'll go alone into the air lock, remember I've been there already and nothing happened to me. I won't touch a thing until that plate you've put on has been sealed behind me, with just a phone connection through it so that I can report. Do you see? There is absolutely no danger—I'll stay in the ship after I have reported, stay there as long as is necessary . . ."

"Going to solve the world's problem all by yourself?" Perkins asked coldly.

"It's out of the question," Chabel said. "There is nothing more to be discussed, the decision has been made."

"We can't abide by that decision, this is too important——"

"You're beginning to sound hysterical," Perkins said. "You see what I said, Professor Chabel, this man can't be relied on."

"I can't be relied on?" Sam said angrily. "That's very funny coming from you, Eddie. You're not big enough for McKay's shoes and for the general welfare I suggest that you resign. Have you told Professor Chabel that you refused to take action on Nita Mendel's report about Rand-gamma in dogs——"

"That's enough, Doctor!" Chabel interrupted angrily.

"I was afraid this would happen," Perkins said, not looking

at Sam. "That was why I warned you. He has made these charges in private and I have ignored them, but now he has made them in public and something must be done."

"Something will have to be done about you, Eddie—not me," Sam said, controlling his burning anger only with the greatest effort. "You've bungled and you've lied to cover it up. You may be a good surgeon but you are a lousy administrator."

They both ignored him; Chabel turned to the intercom and pressed it. "Would you have the officer come in now?"

It was going too fast for Sam and he did not realize what was happening until the office door opened and the police lieutenant walked in.

"I don't want to do this," Chabel said, "but things . . . events leave me with no alternative. I'm sorry, Sam, and I hope you'll understand. The lieutenant is not arresting you, it's just preventative detention. You've forced us to do it. There are irresponsible people who might listen to you and infinite harm could be caused if any attempt were made to enter the spaceship."

Sam stopped listening. He turned and walked toward the door, head lowered and feet dragging, hoping that they had forgotten one thing, and stopped at the open door as the lieutenant took his arm. They *had* forgotten. Other than the secretary the outer office was empty. The lieutenant, fortyish and slightly balding, had come alone to arrest a doctor who had opinions different from other doctors, a political charge that could be enforced under martial law. Sam turned to face the room behind him.

"Thanks, Eddie," he said, and kept turning.

They had forgotten that for almost ten years he had been a combat infantryman.

The lieutenant had not been expecting any trouble; he was off balance and unready. Sam levered on the policeman's wrist, twisting expertly in a punishing armlock that spun the man about and jarred him off balance just as Sam's lowered shoulder slammed into the middle of his back. He stumbled across the room and smashed into the white-faced Eddie Perkins—Sam had a last glimpse of them falling together as he closed the door and went quickly by the frightened secretary and into the hall.

How long did he have? The hall was empty and as he ran down it he tried to figure out what to do next. There was no time to panic or just to run, they would be after him

93

within seconds. And no time to wait for an elevator—he pushed through the door to the fire stairs and went down them five at a time. *No time to break a leg, either!* With an effort he slowed down, then pushed open the door two floors lower down. There were people here and he walked slowly along the corridor and through the swinging doors into the old wing, to a different bank of elevators.

What next? The policeman would have rushed out into the hall to try and catch him, then returned when he found Sam gone. Neither Perkins nor Chabel would have had the presence of mind to do anything while the lieutenant was out. Then the cop would take charge. They were phoning now, probably to the police guard on the main entrance, then to the other entrances, then finally there would be a hospital-wide alarm. The police would be waiting at his room too; he couldn't change clothes, so even if he got outside the hospital how far could he get in these whites? The elevator doors opened before him and he stepped forward.

"What have you been doing, Sam—running the mile? You're all in a sweat."

Dr. Con Roussell walked into the elevator behind him.

"You should know, Con, we were out in the meat wagon together."

"I lost track of you after we got to the bridge, what a night it was! What happened?" The doors closed and Roussell punched his floor, the twenty-third Sam noticed, the residential floor above his own.

"A lot's been happening. For one thing Nita—Dr. Nita Mendel has Rand's."

"The hell you say! The girl with the red hair that was with you at the 'Pericles'?" They came out of the elevator, walking together.

"Yes, that's the one. Everything is going to pieces and the end is nowhere in sight. Do you have any Surital? I'm going to try and get a few hours' sleep."

"Sure, in my room—but don't you have any in your bag?"

"Empty. And I'm not up to trotting along to the pharmacy for more."

Sam closed the door as Roussell unlocked the wardrobe and took out his bag and rummaged through it. "Are you sure you don't want Noctec or something like that?" he asked, coming up with the charged hypodermic needle.

"I drink that like mother's milk," Sam said, taking the needle. "A few cc's of this and I'll sleep like a babe."

"Take more than six and you'll be under for twenty-four hours," Roussell said, turning away. Sam slapped Roussell with the needle, right through his shirt, and emptied the barrel into his arm.

"Sorry, Con," he said, holding the man until he stopped struggling and sank to his knees. "This way you'll be in no trouble for aiding and abetting—and you'll get a good night's sleep, which you need."

He quickly dragged the other intern to the bed, then locked the door. By happy chance both of them were almost the same size and the clothes would fit well enough. Sam stripped and dressed in a one-piece blue suit with a little leather-string necktie, which was so popular these days. It was still raining so he put a raincoat envelope into the black bag before he picked it up and went out.

While he dressed he had been thinking, making his mind up as to which would be the safest way out of the giant hospital. More than twenty minutes had elapsed since he pushed over the cop, time enough to alert all the guards at the main entrances. But there were other entrances, to the clinics and kitchens, that were normally neither guarded nor locked. But which one? More police would have arrived by now and would be assigned to the various entrances as fast as they could be checked off on the floor plan of the hospital. That meant he could use none of them safely, but must find a way to leave that they would not think of until they had sealed all the doors.

He knew where he was going, and was sure he could get out that way, and he could be caught only if he met someone who both knew him by sight and was aware that the police were looking for him. To minimize the chances he went through the new X-ray clinic, not opened yet to the public, and down a back stairs in one of the older buildings. There was no one in sight when he reached the hall on the first floor, slipped on the raincoat, then eased the window open. A few weeks earlier some children had pried this window open and broken into the hospital, and when they had been caught had told how they had got in. The window faced on an alley and was not too far above the ground. No one saw Sam as he swung his legs over the sill, closed the window behind him, then dropped carefully to the ground below.

Now he was out—but what was he to do? His plans didn't extend past this moment; everything he had done had been almost instinctive flight until now. They had tried to capture him and he had resisted, knowing that they were wrong and that the ship *had* to be investigated. The "Pericles," that was still the most important thing, and there was one man who could help him.

General Burke, UNA.

The rain was still falling in steady sheets, blown into eddies on the windy corners, and he was grateful to it since the streets were almost deserted and it gave him some cover. He hurried down Thirty-fourth Street—the rain was also a good excuse for his haste—and turned into the first open bar. It was one of the new, automated, we-never-close kind and, though empty of customers, it had not been shut down. The door opened automatically for him and he headed toward the phone booth in the rear.

"Good morning, sir. A little wet out today, isn't it."

The robot bartender behind the bar nodded toward him, industriously polishing a glass, the perfect picture of the pink-jowled and bald barkeep—though if you leaned far enough over the bar you could see that it was only a torso that ended at the waist. Research had proven that customers, particularly the more inebriated ones, preferred even an imitation man to a flat-faced machine.

"A double Scotch whiskey," Sam said, stopping at the bar. Now that the hurried escape was over he was feeling the fatigue again. He couldn't remember the last time he had slept: alcohol would carry him a bit longer.

"Here you are, sir, a double it is."

The robot poured the glass to the top, full, with a convex meniscus bulging above the rim: at least robots didn't spill the drinks. Sam handed over a bill. "I'll need some small change for the phone."

"Change it is, sir, the customer is always right."

Sam finished his drink then closed himself in the phone booth. Where was it Burke had said he had his HQ, Fort Jay, was that in the Bronx? No, of course not, it was on Governors Island, he must be tired if he couldn't remember that. He called book information and the computer gave him the number and he dialed it. Instead of Fort Jay the local operator appeared.

"I'm sorry, but the number you are trying to reach is a restricted military one. Do you have a priority?"

"No, this is a personal call. Isn't there any way I can call without a priority?"

"Yes, I can connect you to police headquarters on Centre Street, you can explain to them . . ."

"No, thank you—it's not that important." He disconnected at once, then realized that he was sweating. Either the Fort Jay numbers had been on priority for a while—or someone had thought fast and moved even faster. It didn't matter which because the result was the same; it meant it wasn't going to be easy to get in touch with the general. Time was ticking away steadily—and Nita's life was running out.

There was another possibility—the call might have been traced and the police could be on their way here now. Sam hurried out in the driving rain and turned west on Thirty-fourth Street; there were other people in the street now, not many, but enough to give him some concealment. How did he contact Burke? By going to Governors Island, there was no other way. The tunnel was sure to be guarded but he would worry about that after he reached the Battery, where the tunnel entrance was. Getting there was the immediate problem. It was about three miles and he could walk it easily enough, but a lone pedestrian was sure to be spotted and stopped by the police. There were no cabs, and the subways were now running only one automated train an hour. Steal a car? He didn't know how to go about it. When he reached Lexington Avenue he stopped under the monorail as he noticed a flicker of motion from uptown—a train was coming! Then he was running for the station escalator and pelting up the steps as fast as he could. If he caught this train before anyone realized that he had escaped from the hospital he might stay ahead of the search!

When he ran across the station the train had stopped and the doors were already open; he jammed coins into the slot and pushed through the entrance, but he was too late—the doors were starting to close. Fully automated, without a driver or a conductor, the train was leaving as soon as the controls sensed that there was no one waiting to board.

"Wait!" he shouted angrily—and senselessly—as he ran across the platform. He would never make it in time.

There was a thin girl, the only passenger in the car, and she looked up when he called, then put her hand out between the almost-closed doors. They sprang open and before they could shut again Sam was inside.

"Thanks," he said, out of breath, as he dropped into a seat.

"That's all right, you'll do the same for me someday." She

stood and went to the other end of the car and sat down there, facing away from him. People didn't get too close these days.

The buildings swept by soundlessly outside, the rain lashed across the window. Sam opened his collar and dabbed away some of the sweat. Once he opened the black bag and looked inside, then slammed it shut without taking anything out. He was tired—but not that tired yet. If he was going to take any chemical stimulation, it would be best to wait until a time when he would really need it. The jointed silver tube of the monorail train rushed downtown.

There was a stop at Wall Street and Sam got off there, the girl watching impassively as he left. No one else emerged from the train and he was alone on the platform, looking down at the narrow and empty canyons of the streets. The business heart of New York, the financial center of North America, empty and deserted in the middle of the day. He bent his shoulders into the driving rain and walked south.

There were police all around the entrance to the tunnel, a squad car parked in a side street and guards on the platform where the small, remote-controlled busses departed for the island. Sam huddled back into a deep doorway and watched the entrance a block away. Had the police been here all the time—or was this all for his benefit? If it was he had better start moving, it wasn't safe near here. A truck came out of the tunnel and went on without stopping; one policeman waved to it, the only notice they took. Then a staff car appeared, going toward the island and was stopped. Only two officers went over to it but a number of other ones were watching carefully and the barrier remained down. It wasn't until the identity of the driver had been proven that it was allowed to proceed. Sam started to turn away when he saw another vehicle coming out of the tunnel, a jitter—he recognized the high-wheeled, thin outline at once. He should know it, he had been pounded about in one often enough; these airborne jeeps were overpowered and underweight—magnesium, dural, foam rubber—and riding them was like no other experience in this world. Only the UN Army used them.

Sam eased away from the doorway and as soon as he was out of sight of the tunnel entrance he began to run. Where would the jitter be going? Probably north, uptown—but to the East or West Side—or to the local streets? He had to catch it before it reached the first junction—he ran harder, the breath tearing in his throat.

98

When he turned the corner the jitter had already passed—but was waiting at the streetlight while the driver idled the engine, his foot on the clutch. Training—for once he loved it. The streets were empty but the man still stopped for the light. There was an officer seated next to the driver.

"Wait! Over here!" Sam shouted as the light changed and the jitter surged forward. The driver automatically applied the brake when he heard the shout and the officer turned, his .75 recoilless machine pistol pointed at Sam.

"I'm a doctor!" Sam called, waving the black bag. Perhaps it might help. The officer said something out of the side of his mouth and the machine wheeled around in a tight circle and rolled toward Sam. The muzzle of the gun stayed trained on him.

"What do you want?" the officer asked, a young second lieutenant, hard and thin, but still young.

Sam looked at the lieutenant's shoulder patch, the familiar battered dove with an olive branch in its beak and a crutch tucked under its wing, and he couldn't help smiling.

"You're with the Fifth Airborne so you must know Cleaver Burke . . ."

"Are you referring to General Burke? Make it fast, what do you want?" The lieutenant poked the gun in Sam's direction. He was tired and on edge. And Sam had to convince him quickly; a police car might pass at any moment and would certainly stop to see what was happening this close to the tunnel. He leaned closer to the lieutenant with his face expressionless as he spoke through his barely open mouth.

"General Burke is 'Cleaver' to his friends, Lieutenant—but *only* to close personal friends. Do you understand that? I want you to bring him a message from me." Sam opened his bag and reached for a pad of prescription forms, ignoring the gun that swung to cover his movements.

"Why should I bring any messages for you . . ."

"Because I've asked you to, and Cleaver is waiting for this message—and just what do you think would happen to you if Cleaver didn't get it?"

Sam wrote swiftly without looking up; the silence grew taut.

Cleaver—I've changed my mind. We're going into it. Having trouble. Have boat pick me up land end pier 15 East River. Capt. Green

"I won't be going back to the island for an hour at least, sir," the lieutenant said, and Sam knew he had won. The officer's tone was the same, but the Sir made all the difference.

"That will do fine." Sam folded the note and handed it to him. "For your own sake, Lieutenant, I suggest that you do not read this message nor show it to anyone other than General Burke. That will be the best for everyone."

The officer buttoned it into his breast pocket without a word and the jitter buzzed away. Even if the man did read it, it wouldn't mean much—to anyone but Cleaver. The signature was meaningless—but the rank was his old one and the lieutenant would describe him. If the note reached Cleaver they would come for him at once.

It was ten now and it would be physically impossible for the boat to be there before eleven at the very earliest. Sam began to work his way north slowly, keeping a careful eye out for moving cars. Two patrol cars passed, but both times he saw them well in advance. In one of the doorways where he took shelter he found an open garbage can and he buried the black bag under the rubbish in it. The alarm would be out for him by now and anything that marked him as a doctor had to be avoided. On Maiden Lane, within sight of the gray water of the East River, a robot bar was doing a good business; it takes more than a plague to keep sailors out of a saloon and the place was half full. Sam ordered a roast beef sandwich, there were still some in deep freeze, and a bottle of beer from the robot bartender—it was tricked out in an unwholesomely cute pirate eye patch and neckerchief—and ate slowly. By eleven he was walking along the waterfront looking for a secure spot where he could wait. There were some heavy crates next to the warehouse on pier 15 at the foot of Fletcher Street, and by hunkering down between them he was concealed from sight on the land side. It was wet and uncomfortable but he had a good view of the slip, although the end of the pier was half concealed by fog and falling rain.

There was the sound of heavy motors as an occasional ship passed, but too far out for him to see in the mist. Once a louder hammer of an engine drew his attention and he pulled himself further back between the boxes as a river police launch rumbled by, sweeping close to the end of the pier but not turning into the slip. By noon he was soaked through and getting bitter, and by one o'clock he was thinking of the eighty different things he would like to do to the pinheaded lieutenant if he ever saw him again.

At exactly 1:13 the silent shape of a small recon boat swung into the slip and coasted toward him with only the slightest burble of sound coming from its underwater hydraulic jets. Standing in the bow was the lieutenant. Sam pulled himself to his feet, stiff and cramped, and the boat nosed in his direction.

"If you knew what I have been thinking about you——" Sam said, and smiled.

"I don't blame you, sir," the lieutenant said, chewing nervously at his lower lip as he held out his hand to help Sam off the ladder. "I was less than an hour getting back to the tunnel, but there was some kind of trouble there with the police and everything was jammed up. It was only about a half an hour ago that I got through and brought your note to the general. You were right, sir," he tried a tentative smile. "I've never seen him act like that before, not even in combat. He went up like an A-bomb and he got this boat from somewhere and had it in the water and me and the coxswain and all in it, inside of ten minutes."

"Here we go," the coxswain said, opening the throttle and turning in a tight circle. Sam and the lieutenant moved into the bow to get some protection from the low windshield and, at the same moment, they saw the river police launch nose around the end of the pier and head toward them.

"Get down!" the lieutenant said, but Sam had already dropped onto the deck, sheltering behind the low sides. "Get under that tarp."

The T5 coxswain in the stern kicked a bundled up tarpaulin toward Sam without looking down as he did it, and it stopped at the ammunition boxes in the waist. Sam wriggled over to it, drew it toward him and struggled to open it without rising high enough to be seen: he could hear the launch rumbling closer. The stiff canvas resisted and in desperation he kicked hard into the folds with his feet and pulled it up over him. With his knees against his chest he could just about fit under the unrolled part and the last thing he saw as he pulled his head under was the lieutenant turning to face the police boat and resting his fingers, by chance, on the trigger guard of his machine pistol.

"Stop your engine . . . what are you doing here?" an amplified voice bellowed across the narrowing stretch of water.

101

"Keep it moving, slow as you can," the lieutenant said, just loudly enough for the coxswain to hear. Sam sweated under the stifling cover, unable to move or to see the launch swinging closer. "Official business," the lieutenant shouted across the water.

"What do you mean?" The launch was so close now that they had abandoned the bullhorn. "Catch this line, we want to search you."

Sam controlled his involuntary movement as the rope thudded across the canvas. The lieutenant reached out his foot and kicked it into the water.

"I'm sorry," he said. "This is a unit engaged on active duty and we've just put some equipment ashore and our orders are to return at once."

The launch had stopped and the policemen on deck were all armed: a power turret with quadruple recoilless one-inchers was manned and the barrels depressed. The Army boat, moving slowly, was already past the stern of the other boat. The police sergeant looked down at it angrily.

"Stop at once—that is an order. Or . . ."

"This is a military zone, you cannot issue any orders to me." The lieutenant swung up his machine pistol and aimed it at the launch. "Open her wide when I say good-by," he said in a low voice to the coxswain; then loudly, "If you attempt to restrain us I will open fire. I'm sure you don't want any incidents like that, do you? So let's just say good-by."

A loud burbling sounded under the keel and the boat leaped forward; the lieutenant braced himself against the sudden thrust and kept the gun aimed at the launch.

"Stop there! Stop!" the bullhorn shouted and the launch started to swing about but no shots were fired. Before it had turned all the way the recon boat had cleared the end of the pier and swung downstream. The lieutenant dropped down as they began pounding from wave crest to wave crest.

"Can we outrun them?" Sam asked, throwing off the tarp.

"With one jet plugged," the lieutenant said, holding out a pack of cigarettes. He was smiling easily but his forehead was dotted with drops of sweat as well as rain. "This is one of the new jobs, no armor, no range—but it can beat anything that floats."

Sam took one of the cigarettes and looked back, the dock had vanished in the mist and the launch still hadn't appeared.

"Thanks, Lieutenant . . . ?"

"Haber, Dennis Haber. They call me Dan."

". . . Thanks, Dan. That wasn't so easy."

"It *was* easy, I guarantee it. The general told me to come back with you, or to get you back alone, but if I came back without you . . . listen, you know the general. I would much rather get into a fire fight with the cops any day."

"I think you're right."

They grabbed for handholds as the boat heeled over to miss a buoy, then straightened out toward Governors Island again. The dark shape of the fort was already visible ahead and the coxswain throttled back, heading for a narrow dock that paralled the shore. A jitter was waiting there and its motor ground into life as they approached. Cleaver Burke climbed out of it and helped Sam up from the boat himself, his fingers clamping like pliers.

"I'm glad you changed your mind, Sam—it's about time we had some action over that spaceship. Now, with the right publicity, we can get enough public approval to open it up." Lieutenant Haber went into the front of the jitter while they stepped over the low side into the back.

"It's too late for the publicity, Cleaver. Too much has changed and I—well, I'll tell you when we're alone."

"Alone?" The general lowered his thick eyebrows in the well-known scowl that always meant trouble. "Don't you know where you are? This is *my* unit, *my* driver . . . and Dan there is one of *my* officers. Now bite it out, boy. What's all this cloak-and-dagger nonsense?"

"The police are after me."

"Is that all? They won't arrest you here, hah! Is there any secret why they are after you?"

"They don't want me to get in touch with you."

"Well, they haven't been doing too well." He glanced at Sam out of the corners of his eyes. "And just what is wrong with your getting in touch with me?"

"That should be obvious, Cleaver—they're afraid of trouble and they don't want any interference with Operation Cleansweep."

"Maybe I'm being a little thick today, Sam. What can you or I do that could possibly interfere with Cleansweep?"

"You might cause trouble over the Emergency Council's decision about A-bombing the 'Pericles.'"

"Now isn't that interesting," Cleaver said, and his voice was suddenly very cold. "This is the first time I have heard anything about that."

The jitter bounced to a stop in front of the headquarters

building. "Come up to my office," Cleaver told Sam, then turned to the lieutenant and the driver. "Pass the word along that no civilians have come to this island today and no one here has ever heard of a Dr. Bertolli."

"Yes, sir," Lieutenant Haber said as he saluted. "You'll be alone in your office now, General?"

"You catch on quick, boy. You better hang around the orderly room and take my calls for a while. The corporal here can carry the message back to the dock."

Once inside, with the door closed, Cleaver relinquished his hold on his temper. "Politicians," he snorted, stamping the length of the room. "Meatheads! Sitting up there on their fat duffs and making unilateral decisions that may affect the entire future of the human race—and making those decisions out of fear. I hadn't realized that the old philosophy of a bomb-waving solution for international problems was still lurking in dark, spider-filled corners of the political mind. Cretins! They talk about war on disease without realizing that it *is* a war, particularly now, and has to be run like a war. We need good intelligence and the only place we're going to find it is inside that spaceship. They're operating out of fear—if you can't run away from the unknown, why just blow it up!"

"They seem to be afraid of you too, Cleaver—even though you are under UN command. Why else wouldn't they inform you about the decision to destroy the 'Pericles'?"

The general pulled open a file cabinet and took out a giant, two-quart bottle of bourbon. "Get the glasses out of the desk drawer," he said, then filled the large water glasses almost to the brim. "Are they really afraid I'll bust into that spacer?"

"It looks like it."

"Well—should I? What's the reason *you* want to look at it? What do you think we can find?"

Sam had the glass raised to his lips when he stopped suddenly, frozen, then slowly lowered it, untasted, back to the desk.

He knew what they would find in the ship.

This was no logical conclusion but a leap in the dark as his subconscious put together a number of clues that had been collecting ever since the spaceship had landed. It was a single answer that could explain everything that had happened—yet it was an incredible answer that he did not dare speak aloud if he wanted Cleaver to help him get into the

104

"Pericles." He couldn't tell him this, so he had to fall back upon the general's own arguments.

"We can't possibly know what we'll find in there, Cleaver, though there should surely be records of some kind. The important thing is that we cannot completely ignore the possibility of missing out on anything that might be of help. And there is—well—something else."

"What?"

"I don't know, it's just a guess—a wild hunch—and so wild I don't want to talk about it. But I do know that we *must* get into that ship."

"That's not much to go on, Sam, you realize that? Not now. It would have been enough awhile back when we could have raised a political stink and got some public pressure working on our side to take a look into the ship. But public pressure and publicity are out now and there is only one way left that we can get into that ship . . ." He broke off, swirling the liquor round and round in his glass before drinking the remainder in a long swallow.

"I'll say it so you won't have to, Cleaver. We'll have to break into that rocket by force—in spite of the guards."

When he finally answered, the general's voice was flat and empty of emotion.

"That's treason you're talking about, boy—do you know that? And I'm a serving officer in the Army in a time of international peril. If I did what you're suggesting I could be shot."

"If you don't do it, people are going to keep right on dying by the thousands then by the tens of thousands—because I can guarantee that we're no closer now to finding a cure for Rand's disease than we were the day it started. I took the same oath of allegiance that you did, Cleaver, and I'd break it in an instant if I felt that the people on the top had made a wrong decision over a danger as big as this one. And they *have* made a wrong decision . . ."

"I know they have—but it's asking too much, Sam! I agree the ship should be entered, but I can't bring myself to do it this way, not with the slight evidence, guesses and hunches that we have——"

A light knocking on the door interrupted him and he threw it open angrily. "What the devil do you want?" he asked Lieutenant Haber, who was uncomfortably standing there.

"I'm sorry, sir, I've been turning away all the calls and

people who wanted to see you but—there is a call on the hot line, I didn't feel qualified to take it."

General Burke hesitated for a single instant. "That's fine, Haber. Put it through to me here."

He relocked the door then seated himself behind the large desk where there sat three phones, one of them a brilliant red.

"Top secret direct line," he said, picking up the hand set. "Keep out of range of the pickup."

It was a brief conversation, almost a monologue because Burke said little more than yes and no, then hung up. He seemed to have aged a bit and he rested his hands on the desk top as though he were tired.

"It's happened," he finally said. "More cases of the plague, people dropping on the streets. Your labs at Bellevue have confirmed the change."

"You mean that . . ."

"Yes. People can catch it now from one another, it doesn't need the dogs and birds any more. I can see them at the Emergency Council as soon as they hear about this, reaching for their bombs. Just as sure as eggs is eggs they are going to wipe out this plague spot and the few odd million people that happen to be in it at the time, which will probably include you and me."

He stood and tightened his belt.

"We're going to crack that rocket ship 'Pericles' open, boy. That's the only hope we have in hell."

11

General Burke checked the points off on his fingers as he made them.

"First," he said, pushing up his thumb, "we need a military operation, which I trust you will allow me to organize. A small, light force will be the best, I'll lead it myself . . ."

"You shouldn't get personally involved in this," Sam said.

"Horse apples! I'm responsible for this show and I'll be just as guilty giving the orders from the front line as I will be from the rear. Plus the fact that I'm getting too desk bound and I'm hard pressed these days to find any reasons at all to get into the field. So that's set. Second, we need a medical man along since it's medical intelligence that we're after, which will be you. Thirdly, there must be someone who knows something about spaceships, the 'Pericles' in particular, who can get us into it and show us around, and there is a natural choice for that job."

"Stanley Yasumura?"

"Correct. He flew in from California as soon as the 'Pericles' landed and has been bugging everyone since then—myself included—to be allowed to enter the ship. He was one of the principal designers of the 'Pericles' and seems to feel personally responsible for what has happened. I think he'll come with us, but I'll talk to him first and sound him out before I give him any details."

"You can't use the phone, you'll be overheard, cut off."

"We in the military are not without resources, boy. I'll send Haber up to Yasumura's hotel with a command transceiver, one of the new ones fitted with a scrambler and wavelength wobbler, they can't be jammed or eavesdropped. I can handle this part of the operation—will you need any medical kit?"

"No, nothing that I can think of."

"Good. Then your assignment now is to get some sleep so you'll be ready for tonight."

"We can't wait until then!" As he spoke Sam saw Nita's face clearly, sick, silent, unmoving. In the rush of events he had pushed the memory away: it returned with doubled impact now. She was dying minute by minute and there was no time to waste.

"We *have* to wait, Sam, because, aside from the fact that you look like you've been on a ten-day drunk and have given up sleeping as a bad habit, what we have to do can only be done after dark. We can't just walk up to the spacer and climb in. It's surrounded by city police who have orders to shoot anyone crossing the wire. Then there is the covering plate and the air lock to go through—and how much chance do you think we would have in daylight? Plus the fact that it will take awhile to set this operation up. So here's what you do: go into the next room where I have a cot that I use

107

when the work keeps me here. Just take a rest; don't sleep if you don't want to, and you will be able to hear everything that goes on in here. You're going to be no good to us if you're pooped even before the operation begins."

Sam could find no holes in the arguments and the sight of the cot reminded him just how tired he was.

"I'll lie down," he said, "rest a bit. But I don't want to sleep."

Someone had put a blanket over him and through the closed door to the adjoining office came a mumble of voices. Sam jerked awake, sitting up: the room was almost dark and the sky outside the rain-streaked window was murky and gray. He hadn't wanted to sleep but was glad now that he had—it was going to be a long night. When he opened the door the officers around the desk looked up; General Burke put down a blueprint and turned around in his chair.

"You're just in time, Sam, I was going to wake you. We're in the final stages now and it will be dark enough to leave in about an hour. Have you met Dr. Yasumura?"

The circle of soldiers opened up and the small, globular form of the Nisei engineer bounced out, dressed in oversized Army fatigues.

"Hi, Sam, I heard a lot about you." He took Sam's hand and pumped it enthusiastically. "I've been trying to see you ever since I got into town, but you were never available."

"None of the calls reached me, Doctor Yas——"

"Stanley, the name's Stanley, you're the doctor around here, Sam. The general has been telling me about the plot to keep us all apart. He sent an armed guard and a fancy radio to my hotel, then got on it and explained what has been happening—I signed on for the duration. His boys had this uniform for me—wrong size naturally—and even an ID card, so I had no trouble getting here. Now you have to tell me, when you were in the air lock did you——"

"Hold it a moment, Yasumura," General Burke broke in. "Let's take the whole operation in sequence, it wouldn't hurt any of us to run through it once more and we want to brief Sam. Then he can give you the technical advice at the end."

"I just wanted to know——"

"It'll keep. Sit down, Sam, have a drink and look at this map. See where we are now on Governors Island, right in the top of the Upper Bay? From here we have to cross all of the end of Long Island filled with citizens and cops to reach Kennedy Airport, right?" Sam nodded. "Well, there is an easier and a lot less public way to get there—by water." He traced the route with his finger.

"Out through the Narrows and the Lower Bay, then east past Coney Island and in through Rockaway Inlet. We pick our way through Jamaica Bay and come ashore on the end of the airport runway where it sticks out into the water."

"There's only one thing wrong," Sam said, tapping the map. "It must be over thirty miles going this way, we'll be all night in a small boat finding our way through those inlets and marshes."

"No boat, we use a hoverjeep. With all the equipment we're taking it will only hold four, but that's all we need since you, I and Haber can take care of any trouble we run into. All right, we're at the airport now. Haber flew over it in a chopper earlier today—we found him a legitimate excuse. He took pictures and he kept his eyes open. Haber."

The lieutenant tapped the map where the shallow water of the bay touched the edge of the airport. "There are no guards here at all, but in the blown-up prints we found ultra-violet trespass alarms and infrared detectors. Getting by them will be no problem. Trouble starts here, around the 'Pericles,' more detectors and a barbed-wire fence—patrolled by armed police. The real difficulty will be getting by those police guards without raising the alarm. I assume that they will . . . that is, we will want to show discretion about injuring them?" He looked up at General Burke, then glanced quickly away.

There was a lengthening silence as the general looked impassively at the map: someone's shoe scraped as he moved his feet and there was a muted cough.

"We finally come to that, don't we," General Burke said quietly. "We've all fought in a lot of campaigns, with your exception, Dr. Yasumura, and in some odd corners of the world. The Fifth Airborne is an American division so therefore, in keeping with UN policy, we have never been in active service in North America before. We've killed when we had to, when killing was the only way to enforce the peace, and while we have perhaps regretted doing this, we know that many times it has been the only choice. Now we're serving in our own country and the enemy is a handful of average cops who are just following orders on a dull guard detail. I'm beginning to appreciate the UN dictum of never fighting where you're recruiting. All right. Keep the safeties on your weapons, use your blackjacks, but if it comes down to a matter of you or the other guy I want it to be you. We have too much at stake here. Is that understood?"

"It may not be that bad," Sam said. "I'll bring a pressure hypo of Denilin; it's a quick-action sedative that will put a man under in seconds."

"You bring your needle, Sam, and we'll give you every chance to use it. Let's hope it works out that way, and if it doesn't I don't want any of you to forget what you have to do. We pass the guards, get through the wire and reach the spaceship—then what? How do we get in, Dr. Yasumura?"

"Through the air lock, there is no other way. This ship was built to stand up to Jupiter's gravity and atmosphere and there is very little short of an A-bomb that will make a dent in it." He picked up the photograph of the "Pericles" made that morning. "The police cut away the ladder when they welded that plate over the lock—do I hear any suggestions how we can get up those twenty feet from the ground?"

There were a half-dozen officers in the room, men from General Burke's staff, seriously considering the problem of illegal entry of the spaceship. Sam knew that none of them questioned the general's decision to enter it by force; they just did as they were directed with a loyalty given to few officers. Perhaps they wouldn't walk off a cliff if the general demanded it, but they would certainly follow him if he went first.

"What's the hull made of?" a graying captain of engineers asked.

"A specially developed titanium alloy; it contains no iron."

"Then magnets are out. Our longest folding ladder is just fifteen feet——"

"Then bolt an extension on the end," General Burke interrupted. "We have very little time left, let's get on with this. We're on the ladder now, standing in front of that plate they welded on—how do we get through that?"

"No problem, General," the engineer said. "You'll carry one of the portable lasers we use for cutting heavy metal in the field. I understand that plate is made of mild steel, the laser will cut it like butter."

"Now we're moving along; we're in the air lock and that's where you take over, Dr. Yasumura."

"I will need tools, a multitester, portable scope and some things like that. I've talked this over with your engineers and they'll give me everything I need. There are only one or two ways that Commander Rand could have disconnected the controls so that the inner door will not open, and once I crack into the control box there I'll find out and open it up. Once we're through that door we'll go through the ship from bow to stern until we find what Rand meant when he wrote *sick in ship*. And I'll find the log, see how the ship handled during the landing, the equations——"

"Just try to control your technical enthusiasm until you get there, Yasumura, we're not in the ship yet. I suggest you get what gear you need from the engineers so it can be loaded into the jeep. Lieutenant Haber will go with you to draw the antidetector units. Sergeant Bennett will get some coffee and sandwiches up here. Dismissed."

The first trouble came fifteen minutes later.

"Sorry, sir, but we can't get all the equipment into the hoverjeep," Haber reported.

"Lieutenant, you're an idiot. Stuff it in, boy—stuff it in!"

"Yes, sir. What I mean is we can't get in the equipment and four passengers and get the thing off the ground. There just isn't enough power."

"We'll take two jeeps then, and if we can we'll squeeze in another man to help carry that gear."

"That will be me, sir," Sergeant Bennett said.

"Agreed. Get into night fatigues and bring a can of blackface."

Sodium vapor lights sliced the darkness of the yard, illuminating the falling rain with their crackling blue glow and casting black shadows under the cigar-box bodies of the hoverjeeps that rumbled and whistled noisily as they floated a yard above the ground, supported on the cushion of air blasted downward by their fans.

"Drop them!" General Burke shouted. Like the others of the raiding party he was dressed in black coveralls and dark boots with a black beret pulled low over his hair. Their faces, hands and visible skin were soot-colored, without highlights, stained by the blackface cream.

"Engine warm, tank full, radio and radar tested, sir," the driver of the first hoverjeep said, switching off and climbing out. "She'll lift, hover and do full speed with this load you're carrying."

"Let's move then. I'll drive the lead jeep, Sam and Yasumura come with me. Haber, take the second and the sergeant will ride shotgun for you. Stay close behind me and be ready to turn southwest as soon as we see the docks on the Brooklyn shore. We're going to start out of here going due east so keep your eye on the compass; I'll be using radar but the compass is all you'll have, that and the sight of my rear end going away from you, so don't get lost. We're going to put on a bit of a show in case the police are using radar too. There are five copters going out with us and they'll fly low and we'll go at maximum altitude so all the blips will merge. When we get in the radar shadow of the shore installations we'll drop down and cut out while the copters fly around for a while. Any questions? All right then, here we go."

The whistling of the fans was drowned out as the flight of copters came over, dropping low. The general signaled and all the lights went out at the same moment; watery darkness filled the yard and the hoverjeeps were invisible as they drifted across the ground and slipped down the ramp to the water. The riding lights of the copters vanished into the falling rain, their unseen companions moving beneath them.

"Shore about two hundred yards ahead," Sam reported, bent over the hooded screen of the radar.

"I can't see a damn thing," the general muttered. "No, I'm wrong, there it is." He touched the switch on the microphone. "Cut in your silencers, be ready to turn—*now!*"

With the silencers engaged, their speed dropped by a third and the copters rumbled away into the darkness. As the two hoverjeeps turned toward the ocean their passage was marked only by the dimpled water that they floated above and the muttering, muted whistle of their fans. Silent jets of air drove them forward, down the Upper Bay and under the briefly glimpsed lights of the Narrows Bridge and into the Lower Bay and the higher waves of the Atlantic. Once they were well away from the shore the silencers were cut out and they tore through the darkness with racing-car speed. The rain was stopping and through patches in the haze they caught glimpses of a row of lights off on their left.

"What's that?" General Burke asked.

"Coney Island, the street and boardwalk lights along the shore," Sam said, squinting at the radar.

"Blast! Just when we could use some filthy weather it has to clear up—what's that I'm coming to ahead?"

"Rockaway Inlet, it leads into Jamaica Bay. Stay on this course, we're in the middle of the channel and we have to go under the bridge that crosses it."

There was no traffic on the bridge that they could see

and it appeared to float in midair, vanishing out of sight into the mist in both directions: they drifted under it with muted fans. Ahead lay the wilderness of mudbanks, waterways, swamps and waving cattails that made up the heart of Jamaica Bay. They floated over it, ignoring the marked channels as the hover craft crossed water, reed clumps and mud flats with equal facility. Then the bay was behind them and just ahead was the straight line of the filled land and the lights marking the end of the Kennedy Airport runway. With engines throttled back they drifted up the bank.

"The alarms begin right there at the lights, sir," Haber's voice whispered in General Burke's earphone.

"Put down then, we'll go the rest of the way on foot." They dropped like silent shadows and the men climbed out and unloaded the equipment. "Sergeant, you've had the most experience with the cheaters; we'll hold here while you put them in."

Sergeant Bennett shouldered the heavy equipment pack and crawled forward in the mud, the detector rod held out before him. They could see nothing of his advance and Sam held his impatience under control and tried to keep his thoughts off Nita back there in the hospital dying by degrees. He wished that he had put in the cheaters, though he knew that they must have changed in the ten years since he had last handled one. Trying to picture what Bennett was doing would keep his mind off that hospital bed. The swinging prod cutting a regular arc over the ground, then the twitch of the needle on the glowing dial. Knocking out the infrared detectors wasn't difficult, as long as you didn't bang them with the insulation hood when you were dropping it over them at the end of the long rod. The ultraviolet alarms were the tricky ones, first making an accurate reading of the output without cutting the beam in order to adjust the cheater lamp. Then the smooth, continuous motion they had practiced so much, moving the tiny UV generator in front of the pickup so that there was no change in the level of received radiation. Once it was in position you could break the original beam to the photocell because the cheater light was shining into it from a few inches away. Nita, Nita. The minutes stretched out and the air cleared, stars broke through above them. At least there was no moon.

A silent figure loomed up before them and Sam's hand automatically found the butt of his pistol. It was Sergeant Bennett.

"All in position, sir, a pushover, dead easy. If you'll all walk behind me single file I'll take you through the gap."

They went carefully, one behind the other, treading as lightly as they could with the heavy packs and the ladder. The infrared detectors were ignorant of their passage since their body heat was shielded from the pickups by the insulating covers, and though they cut through the invisible beam of ultraviolet light there was no alarm since the cheater fed its own steady UV source guarding photocell.

"That's the last of them," Haber said. "There's nothing now between us and the guards around the ship."

"No cover either," General Burke said, "and the rain has stopped. We'll stay in the grass here and parallel the runway. Keep low and keep quiet."

With its attendant rows of lights the wide runway stretched away from them, terminating suddenly in the dark bulk of the spaceship that sprawled across it, blocking it. A few lights on the ground near the ship marked the location of the guarded, barbed-wire fence that ringed it, but there were black gaps in between the lights. The general led them toward the nearest patch of darkness, midway between two of the lights, and they crawled the last hundred yards on their stomachs. They dropped into the mud, motionless, when a slowly plodding policeman appeared in the nearest illuminated circle. He cradled a recoilless .75 submachine gun in the crook of his arm. No one moved as the guard squelched by them, a dimly moving form against the night sky. Only when he had passed through the next circle of light did General Burke issue his whispered instructions.

"Bennett—knock out the detectors and as soon as you do we can cut through the wire. Sam and Haber move toward that light and get ready to take out any cops that come this way. Yasumura, lie still and shut up. Let's go."

For Stanley Yasumura this was the worst time, just waiting, unable to do anything as the minutes ticked by. The clifflike bulk of the "Pericles" loomed over him and he tried to study it, but there was little to see. The general and the sergeant were working as a team, neutralizing the different alarms. The other two seemed to have vanished in the darkness and all he could do was lie there, plastered with mud and soaked to the skin, and try not to hear the racing thud of his heart. There was a stir of movement at the far side of the nearest light and another policeman appeared, walking steadily toward the spot where Yasumura lay, approaching with measured, heavy steps. It seemed incredible to Yasumura that the man couldn't see him lying there, or that he hadn't heard the rustling movements of the two others working their way toward the barbed wire. And where were the ones who were supposed to be on guard?

In unvoiced answer to his question the two figures rose behind the policeman and closed with him in a silent rush. Haber had his arm about the cop's neck so that the incipient shout became only a muffled gasp, while Sam held his flailing arm, twisting it so that it was palm up and pressing the nozzle of the pressure hypodermic against the bare skin. There was a brief hissing that blasted droplets of the sedative through the skin into the tissue below. For a few seconds there was a soundless struggle as both men held the policeman's writhing figure so that he could not raise an alarm or reach the trigger of his gun: then he collapsed and they eased him to the ground.

"That's fine," General Burke said, appearing out of the darkness. "Lay him over here and take his weapon; we're ready to go through the wire. Pick up the ladder and the rest of the gear and follow me."

"The second strand up from the bottom is carrying a charge," Sergeant Bennett said, pointing to it where it was stapled to the tall wooden pole: the wire fence stretched ten feet above the ground. "I've jumped it with an insulated wire so we can get through, but don't touch the ends."

The wire cutter clicked loudly in the night and they eased the cut sections back.

"That's enough—let's go," Burke said when the wire had been cut up to three feet above the ground.

They crawled under, one at a time, passing the packs through the gap before them. Then they were skirting the base of the towering black ship, picking their way over the broken ground and, as they came around the bulge of a gigantic fin, they saw in the light of the distant hangars the still-open outer door of the air lock.

"Ladder!" the general hissed, and Haber stood it up beneath the door and switched it on. The two small motors, with their power packs, were built into the bottom of the legs; they whined softly and the ladder extended until the top touched just below the lock. Sam had shouldered the heavy-duty batteries and converter unit that powered the laser that Yasumura carried and, while the others steadied the ladder, he followed the engineer to the air lock.

"Plug this in," Yasumura whispered, and handed the end of the cable to Sam. The laser was a milk-bottle-sized tube with a flaring, bell-shaped mouth that automatically spaced the output lens at the correct distance from the work while it shielded the operator's eyes from the fierce light. He put the open end against the large sheet of half-inch steel that had been welded over the lock and switched on the power. It hummed loudly, too loudly in the quiet night, and when he moved it along slowly a black line appeared in the steel: there was the acrid smell of burned metal.

The laser cut steadily and surely, marking a yard-wide circle in the covering plate. Yasumura didn't complete the circle; when it was almost finished he made an adjustment on the laser, then did the last few inches at the bottom. This time the intense beam of monochromatic light did not cut the steel, heating it instead to a cherry red. He turned off the laser and pushed his shoulder against the plate. The ladder swayed and Sam reached up and braced the engineer's legs. Yasumura tried again and slowly the heated hinge bent and the disk of metal leaned inward; he climbed higher and put more weight on it until it was bent almost parallel with the inside floor. He stepped carefully over the still-hot edge and vanished inside.

"Up we go," General Burke said, and Haber started slowly up the ladder under the weight of the heavy pack of equipment.

"If you please, sir," Sergeant Bennett said, "I think I can do more good right here on the ground. If any police come by, I might be able to keep them quiet—the doctor gave me his hypodermic. You need all the time you can get."

Burke hesitated only a fraction of a second. "You're right, Bennett. Rear guard and take care of yourself, no foolish chances."

"Yes, sir." He saluted and moved off toward the opening in the wire.

When the general climbed through the hole in the covering plate he had to brush aside the heavy folds of blackout cloth that the others were fixing across it, and once he was inside the edges were sealed and the battle lamp turned on. They blinked in the sudden light and Yasumura hurried over to the control panel, rubbing his hands together happily. The airlock controls were dead, just as they had been when Sam first tried them, so the engineer began at once to remove the covering panel.

116

"Is this the phone you used?" the general asked.

"It's the one," Sam said, and began running through the numbers. They were connected to compartment after compartment, all empty just as before.

"No signs of anyone, or any kind of disturbance," Burke said, scratching at his blackened jaw. "Try the control room again. Nothing there either. This is a puzzler, Sam."

There was a muffled clang and they turned to see that Yasumura and Haber had lowered the heavy plate to the floor, exposing the interior of the junction box. The engineer probed with a circuit tester, then probed again. He shorted two terminals with the jaws of a pliers and the frown deepened on his forehead.

"That's strange," he said. "There doesn't seem to be any power through this box at all. I can't understand it. Maybe Rand rigged some kind of device inside the ship to break all the current past the inner door once he had opened the outer one. A timing device of some kind, perhaps."

"You mean that you can't open the door?" Burke snapped.

"I didn't say that, it's just difficult . . ."

"What about the power pack from the laser, will that give you enough current for what you need?"

"Of course! I'm eight kinds of idiot for forgetting that. It's more than we need, in fact I'll have to cut down the——"

His voice broke into a mumble as he opened the power pack and changed connections quickly, then ran two wires from it to the open junction box on the wall.

"Here goes!" he said as he closed a relay with an insulated screwdriver.

Nothing happened.

General Burke's voice crackled like sheet lightning. "Well —can you open it or can't you?"

"It should be opened now—but it's not, something has been disconnected inside the ship."

"Then forget the electricity; isn't there any other way through that door—or maybe the wall?"

"You have to understand the construction of this ship, General. Since this air lock was designed to be opened to the Jovian atmosphere, it is just as strong as the rest of the hull. The inner lock is thick as a bank-vault door and twice as tough."

"Are you trying to tell me that—after all we have done to get here—that you can't get us into the bloody ship?"

From somewhere outside there came the sudden hammer

117

of a machine gun and the clang of bullets on the hull. Even as they were turning, a light was focused on the opening they had cut in the metal, a beam strong enough to show through the thick weave of the blackout cloth.

12

The light was on for only a fraction of a second, then vanished as there was a burst of firing from beneath the ship.

"That tears it," Burke said. "They know we're here and our time is cut to nothing. Bennett won't be able to hold them off very long. Get us into the ship, Yasumura . . ."

Another light came on and at the same instant a line of holes stitched itself across the cloth and death screamed and ricocheted around the compartment as half-inch, armor-piercing slugs clanged off the impenetrable metal of the walls. It lasted less than a second, then there was more firing outside and the light was gone. Darkness enveloped the lock as the battle lamp shattered, and in the sudden silence that followed there was a single, choked-off moan.

A tiny cone of light sprang out from Yasumura's penlight, sweeping across Lieutenant Haber lying sprawled out on the floor with blood soaking out through the leg of his coveralls. Sam cut the cloth away quickly and began to dress the wound with his first-aid pack.

"Is there anyone else hurt?" he said.

"I'm fine," the general snapped. "Yasumura—what about you?"

"There is no trouble—listen, we could close the outer port, would that help?"

"Keep us from being shot to death," Burke grunted, "and buy us some time—now you're beginning to think."

"The outer door isn't a problem," the engineer mumbled around the light he clutched in his teeth as he swiftly changed the connections in the junction box. "The motor for it is here as are the wires, so——"

A relay sparked as he closed it and there was the loud-pitched whine of an electric motor in the wall.

"It should be closing——" His words were cut off as another burst of firing tore the cloth covering from the opening and a shaft of burning light poured in. This time there was no answering fire from below and the light remained on. They dropped to the floor and saw the massive door outside swinging slowly toward them. More shots boomed out, a continuous fire, but it was aimed at the closing door not at the open lock. Bullets roared against the metal, screaming away in vibrating ricochets and still the door kept moving, coming on until it hit the steel plate over the opening. The plate bent, tore and the motor whined louder in the wall, then suddenly stopped. The plate had buckled and jammed leaving an opening just a few inches wide.

"The circuit breakers blew when the motor overloaded," Yasumura said.

"It's good enough." General Burke stood up. "Now, how do we get the inner door opened? Can we cut through it with the laser?"

"We could—but it wouldn't do much good. This door is sealed like a bank vault. A motor-powered ring gear inside the door turns pinion gears that drive out three-inch thick bars into sockets in the housing. We can't cut them one by one."

"The trouble then," Sam asked, "is that something is stopping the current from getting to this motor in the door?"

"Yes——"

"Well, couldn't you cut an opening in the door big enough to reach through and connect the motor to the power pack? Then you could move it as you did the outer door . . ."

"Sam, you're wasted in medicine," Yasumura shouted enthusiastically, "because that's just what we're going to do." He began to draw on the sealed door with a grease pencil. "Here are the bars, the ring gear . . . and the motor should be about here. If we cut through at this spot we should miss the motor, but be in the central cavity where we can wire into it."

He threw down the pencil and began to pull the wires from the power pack and to reconnect it. There were more shots from outside, but none of them found the narrow slot of the doorway. The laser buzzed and Yasumura pressed it to the door over the spot he had marked.

It was slow work. The metal of the door was dense and resistant and the laser cut only a fraction of an inch at a time as he worked it in a slow circle the size of a saucer. He finished the circle and went over it again to deepen it. The metal heated and stank. General Burke crawled over to the door, shielded his eyes from the light and tried to see out, then put his gun to his shoulder and fired a burst. He dropped low as the firing was returned and the lock rang like a bell with the impact of the slugs on the massive door.

"They're bringing up a fire engine with a tower. I scattered them a bit. But they'll bring it back again or someone will think to use a high-pressure hose and they'll wash us out of here. How is it coming?"

"I should have cut through by now," Yasumura gasped, leaning on the laser, "but this metal . . ." There was a clatter as the plug of metal dropped free.

"Now open it!" Burke snapped and fired another burst through the gap.

It was slow, painful work teasing the plug of metal out of the hole far enough to get a grip on it with a wrench. Sam stood ready, clamped down quickly as soon as he could and pulled the hot cylinder from the hole, throwing it the length of the air lock. Heedless of his smoldering sleeve, Yasumura flashed the light into the opening.

"There it is!" he chortled. "Bang on. Pass me the long-shanked screwdriver and the cables from the power pack."

Attaching the wires at the bottom of the deep hole was exacting work, made even more difficult by the hot metal that burned into the little engineer's flesh. Sam could see the angry welts rising on his skin and the way he bit hard on his lip while beads of sweat sprang out on his face.

"Done . . ." he gasped, and pulled the screwdriver out. "Turn on the power, the motor is hooked up."

There was an angry whirring buzz from the opening that lasted almost a minute and, when it rose in frequency, Yasumura switched the electricity off. He squinted in through the opening with the light.

"The rods are withdrawn, so let's see if we can push this thing open!"

They heaved against the door's unyielding bulk, planting

their feet on the deck and straining until their muscles cracked. It didn't move.

"Once more—" Burke gasped, "and this time give it everything."

With their lips drawn back from their clenched teeth they strained at the massive door and Haber dragged himself across the floor and struggled up on one leg to add his weight to the effort.

Slowly, with reluctant motion, it moved inward.

"Keep it going . . ." the general gasped as the gap widened, first a fraction of an inch, then more, until light streamed out and it was big enough to get through. "That's enough . . . !"

Sam eased the wounded lieutenant back to the deck as Burke slid cautiously through the gap with his gun pointed before him. He lowered it and laughed brusquely.

"I don't think it's much good for shooting germs. Come on, all of you in here and bring the equipment."

They handed it in through the opening, then Sam helped Haber to his feet and passed him through to Burke before squeezing past the door himself.

"Look at that," Yasumura said, pointing to a jagged, smoke-stained opening in the wall of the corridor. "That's where the junction box for the air-lock controls used to be. There must have been a charge of explosive in there— it would have been simple enough for Rand to rig that with a time fuse. But why . . . ?"

"That's what we're here to find out," Burke said. "Haber, you're not so mobile, so stay here as rear guard and see to if no one gets in to bother us."

"Yes, sir."

"Dr. Yasumura, I imagine the control room would be the best place to look for anything—will you lead the way?"

"Down this connecting corridor, there's an elevator that goes directly there."

He went first and their footsteps echoed loudly in the empty ship. They walked warily, looking into every doorway they passed, cautious although they did not know why.

"Hold it," Yasumura said, and they stopped instantly, guns swinging to the ready. He pointed to a thick insulated wire that crossed the floor of the corridor before them, emerging from a jagged hole in one wall and vanishing into the other. "That cable, it wasn't here when the ship left Earth."

Sam knelt and looked at it closely. "It seems normal

enough, from the ship's supplies I imagine. The 'Pericles' was on Jupiter for almost two years; this must be a modification of some kind that they made there."

"I still don't like it," the engineer said, glaring at the heavy wire suspiciously. "There are cableways between decks, they could have run it there. Better not touch it now, I'll take a closer look at it later."

The destroyed junction box for the air lock seemed to be the only damage that had been done to the ship: the atomic pile was still in operation, the electrical current was on and the air fresh, though it had the canned. odor of constant recycling. When they rang for the elevator its door slid open at once.

"The control room is right up top, in the nose of the ship," Yasumura said, pressing the button. As the elevator hummed up the shaft the tension increased with every passing instant, a spring being coiled tighter and tighter. When the door slid open both Sam and the general had their guns raised and pointed without being aware of it; they stepped out. Some of the tension ebbed as they saw that the domed chamber was as empty of life—or death—as it had been when they had first looked at it on the phone screen in the air lock.

"What the devil.is that?" Yasumura asked, pointing to a foot-square metal box that was welded to the deck against the back wall. "Another new installation since the ship left—I wonder what it is for?"

It was a crude cube made of ragged-edged metal sheets welded together with a wide and irregular bead. Small cables emerged from holes in its sides and a larger, wrist-thick cable came up from the top and vanished through a jagged gash cut into the wall. They traced the smaller cables and found that they ran to the control boards, most of them to the communication equipment. Sam stood in front of the control chairs and faced out into the room.

"That's interesting," he said. "I didn't think I had seen these cables or the box before when I used the phone to look in here—and I didn't. It may be just an accident, but none of them is visible from where I'm standing—right in front of the pickup for the phone."

"Something even more interesting," Yasumura said, pointing. "All of the communicators, long wave, FM, everything— they're all turned on."

General Burke turned slowly, his eyes following the converging wires back to the box, to the heavy cable that ran up the hole in the wall and vanished. "I think we had better take a look and see where that big cable goes to," he said.

"What about the ship's log?" Sam asked. "There should be something about the disease there, or there may be other records."

"They'll keep for the moment," the general said, starting toward the door. "I want to find out first just what is going on with all these wires and connections. Come on."

The next compartment was banked with navigation instruments and the cable writhed across the floor like a dead serpent, then plunged through a cracked opening in the plastic panel of the far wall. They tracked it through two more compartments before it dived through a small doorway and down the spiral steps in the tunnel beyond. Another cable looped down from the ceiling and joined it: both vanished out of sight below.

"This is an emergency stairwell," Yasumura said. "It runs the length of the ship."

Only tiny glow tubes illuminated the steps as they wound their way down, deeper and deeper into the spaceship. Other cables came in through open doorways or through ragged holes cut in the metal wall until there were more than a dozen spiraling down with them, sprawling across the steps. Then the end came, suddenly, as they walked around the turn of the steps where all the cables bunched together and ran out through an open door.

"What's out there?" the general asked, "at this level."

Yasumura frowned at the stenciled number on the wall, then counted off on his fingers: he looked surprised. "Why—there's nothing here, we're in the fuel levels. There should be nothing but tanks out there, empty tanks, the fuel here would have been used up on the outward flight."

They eased out through the door, stepping carefully over the tangle of cables, and faced the white wall into which the cables dived.

"That shouldn't be here!" the engineer said.

There was a chill in the air and Sam leaned over and ran the muzzle of his gun along the wall, knocking off a spray of fine ice crystals. Massive, crudely formed girders ran from the wall to the frame of the ship. There was an ordinary TV phone fixed to the wall above the spot where the cables entered. Yasumura pointed at it.

"That phone shouldn't be here either; there's no phone station at this point. And the number is blank——"

Sam stepped by him and turned the phone on, but the screen remained dark.

"You're going to talk to me whether you want to or not," he said, then waved the others to stand back. Before they could stop him, or even knew what he was doing, he had sighted his gun and fired a short burst at the outer edge of the bundle of cables. The bullets screamed away and two of the insulated cables jumped and were severed.

The phone hummed and the screen came to life.

The Jovian looked out at them.

Down through the hurtling torrents of the atmosphere the bulky form of the "Pericles" dropped, pitting its mass and the thrust of its thundering jets against the gravitational pull of Jupiter and the attacking weight of the dense atmosphere. Screaming winds buffeted it, tried to turn it from its plotted course, but sensitive instruments detected the deviation even as it began and informed the computer: the incandescent finger of an atomic jet flared, then another, making the constant compensations and balances that kept the ship's fall under control. Lightning crackled through the soup-thick atmosphere that was compressed by a gravity almost three times greater than Earth's, while methane and ammonia rain hammered at the rocket's metallic skin.

No echo of the tempest outside penetrated to the control room, where the ordered calm was disturbed only by the distant hum of the air vent and an occasional rustle as one of the three men in the deep chairs changed position and spoke a few words in a low voice. The thick and insulated walls cut off all sound and sight, the few tiny direct-vision ports were sealed and capped, and only one viewscreen held a televised view of the surging atmosphere outside, a dark and roiling cloud mass of no interest. The display on the other screens was far more relevant, the course plot, altitude, speed, radar soundings. The ship fell.

"On course so far without readable deviation," the second officer, Commander Rand, said. "We're going to sit down right in the middle of that iceberg." He was a blond man with a mild expression, and seemed too young for the naval rank of commander, even though it was a technical rank earned by his prowess in the mysteries of computer control. He had programmed this landing precisely and completely, so that now all he had to do was sit back and watch it happen.

"I wish you would not refer to the Reef as an iceberg," First Officer Weeke said with slow Dutch thoroughness. "It is made of ice not as we know it on Earth but instead compacted to an incredible hardness. The radio probes have shown that and we have all the readings to prove this is a solid object on which we can land with impunity——"

"Wind velocity is below a hundred m.p.h. What's the air temperature?" Captain Bramley asked.

"Minus one hundred fifty degrees," Rand said. "Just a few degrees lower than the Reef temperature. We're almost down."

They watched the indicators in silence, alert for the emergency that never came, and in each sweep of their eyes across the crowded boards they rested longest on the trajectory display screen where the red blob of their position was sliding down the white line of the selected course toward the rising bulk of the Reef.

That is what it had been called from the very first, the Reef. There might be other reefs lost in the planet-wide sea of frigid and liquefied gas, but they had not looked for them since there was a limit to the number of radio probes they could expend. This reef, the Reef, had been found by one of the first radar rockets and its position had been exactingly plotted. There had been speculation that it might be floating free in that stupendous ocean but it had turned up exactly on schedule ten hours later when Jupiter's rotation brought it back to the same spot. Once they knew where to look and what to look for a constant watch had been kept on the Reef from where they hung in orbit, and when radar observation proved that it was joined inflexibly to the planet's surface all the later rocket probes were directed to it.

Now they were landing on it. Rocket exhausts lanced down slowing the ponderous "Pericles" almost to a stop, jamming the men deep into their acceleration couches, as radar waves probed the surface below looking for the optimum spot for a landing. Then lateral rockets fired, easing them over as they dropped so that they could come to rest on the flattest surface. Hotter and faster burned the jets digging into the ice and sending out clouds of steam that instantly froze and were whipped away by the ceaseless wind, until finally the great mass was suspended above the surface almost unmoving, dropping at inches a second. In spite of this the ship jarred and creaked as they struck and when the jets went off it was gripped by Jupiter's trebled gravity. The structure of the ship groaned and settled to rest under the load. They were down.

"Feels like we're still decelerating," Rand said, pushing himself painfully forward in the chair.

Captain Bramley did not answer until after he had made a visual check of all the stations and exchanged a few words with the men there. This took less than three minutes since the total complement of the "Pericles" was just forty-one, while only a third of this number were even indirectly involved in the operation of the fully automated ship.

"We're down and in one piece and no one injured," the captain said, sinking back into the chair. "These 3G's are going to be hard to live with."

"We'll only have to take it for a week," Rand said, just as the instrument board went wild.

It was unprecedented and unallowed for in any of the instructions that the computer had ever received and, after running through all the possible solutions in its memory bank within nanoseconds and finding no answers, bank after bank of lights flashed red on the boards. The ship's officers took over then, testing and clearing circuits, fighting to find out the trouble and correct it before they were destroyed. Bit by bit, as urgent messages proved that the hull was sound and that no alien atmosphere was leaking in, they regained some of their composure and began to cross check. There was nothing wrong that they could discover easily since it was the instruments themselves that were acting wildly and producing impossible observations. They cut them out one by one and it was First Officer Weeke who finally located the trouble.

"It is a magnetic field, a tremendous one that must be over ten thousand kilogauss to cause this trouble. It is low down in the ship, near to the ground, near to the ice I should say, since there is no ground here, and it is affecting all the instruments within range. It came on suddenly, an unusual phenomenon."

Just how unusual they discovered two hours later when the affected instruments had been taken out of circuit and a measurement had been made of the interfering field.

"Very simple," Captain Bramley said, staring at the typed sheet that had just emerged from the computer. "It is an incredibly powerful field and we have enough steel in the stern

126

of the ship to be affected strongly by it. The attraction of this field just about equals our maximum thrust under full jet."

"Do you mean . . ."

"Exactly. This field is holding us down and if we try to take off while it is still there we will blow ourselves up. For the present moment at least we are effectively trapped on Jupiter."

"It is impossible phenomena," Weeke protested. "Even if this *onaagenaam* planet is a natural cryogenic laboratory for creating magnetic fields of this strength."

"Perhaps the field is not natural," Captain Bramley said, very quietly, just as the signal lights came on indicating that something was moving against the lower portion of the hull.

There were floodlights in armored housings on the outer hull and over half of these had survived the landing. The captain ran his fingers rapidly over the testing circuits, cut out the damaged units, then switched on all the remaining lights at once.

Outside was eternal night since no visible light from the sun could penetrate the banked clouds and Jupiter's compressed, two-hundred-mile-thick atmosphere, where only the occasional flare of lightning lit the darkness. There was light now, intense burning light that picked out every detail of the icescape and clearly revealed the Jovians.

"They are not what I would call handsome," Weeke said.

There may be a law of natural selection that states that an intelligent creature should have its organs of vision placed high for effectiveness, its organs of locomotion low for mobility and its organs of manipulation at the end of flexible extremities for dexterity. This is a crude description of a man although a much more accurate one of a Jovian. They did look like caricatures of *homo sapiens*, a waddling pack of squashed down, broadened, elephant-hided men with tree-trunk limbs and wrinkled saurian heads.

"The light doesn't seem to be bothering them, sir," Rand said. "You'd think it would blind them."

"It would—if those creases on the top of those neckless heads cover eyes, but we don't know. We don't know anything about these creatures except they seem to have enough intelligence to generate a magnetic field to hold us here. We'll have to find some way of communicating with them."

"Perhaps they are trying to do the same thing," Weeke said, pointing to the screen where a group of the Jovians were near the ship's hull. "They seem to be doing something out there. I cannot see what, since it is outside of the range of

127

the pickup, but it is the area from which we are having the readings of movement against the hull."

"That's the port engine room plating," the captain said, dialing that compartment on the phone. He had just made the connection when the far wall of the engine room rang like a drum. "Turn the pickup around—let me see that wall," he ordered, and the scene swam on the screen and steadied on the featureless gray panel.

With a clang like a monster forging press the wall bulged inward and from the center of the swelling emerged a reddish-green rod, no thicker than a man's thumb and tapering to a blunt point on the end. It penetrated a foot or more into the room and although made of material hard enough to stab through the multiple layers of the specially built and strengthened wall it smoked and changed color in the oxygen atmosphere.

The rod began to move, bending and writhing like a snake.

"Evacuate that compartment!" the captain ordered as he hit the alarm button that began an ear-shattering clanging throughout the ship as the emergency, airtight doors started to close.

It was alive, that was obvious—alien flesh of some Jovian creature that was harder than the hardest steel—yet still sentient and aware. It was burning in the air as they watched the screen, smoking and crumbling yet still moving in that slow questing motion as though seeking something. Then it slithered backward out of the hole and the captain's roar of warning was drowned out as the pressurized, frigid atmosphere of Jupiter blasted in through the hole.

Two men did not escape from the compartment before the mounting pressure sealed the door. It was pure chance that saved the ship. If any other compartment had been holed the thin interior walls would have gone down, the poisonous vapor would have spread through the ventilation system and they all would have been dead. But the engine rooms were provided against flarebacks from the combustion chambers with thicker walls, heavier doors and automatic vent-seals. They held. Metal strained and creaked as the pressure heaved against its surroundings but nothing gave way.

For nine more ship days the Jovians left them alone. Occasionally one could be seen passing but they ignored the ship as though it were not there. Rapid work with the remote handling controls in the engine room—before they chilled too much to become inoperable—managed to slap a patch over the small opening and weld it into place. Heavy beams were placed to support it until the pressure could be lowered enough to permit a space-suited volunteer through the air lock to fix a more permanent and stronger patch. This was completed and the air painfully cleaned of the contaminents that had been blasted in through the hole and the engine room was back in operation. Not that there was anything to be done there, the fierce magnetic field still held the ship immobile.

They tried to communicate with the Jovians. With much labor they manufactured a solid-state, fixed-frequency television transceiver. There were no moving parts and the screen and orthicon were of the nonvacuum Partini type. When the set was completed it was poured full of plastic, then imbedded in a larger cube of plastic so it was completely resistant to any pressure changes. The external manipulators swung it out and placed the device where it could be seen clearly by any passing Jovian. Captain Bramley's loudly amplified voice came from it and his image could be clearly seen on the screen and it was ignored completely. Finally one of the Jovians trod on it accidently and crushed it.

"It looks like they're not interested in talking to us," Rand said, but no one smiled.

On the ninth day the Jovians began to gather again about the ship and as a precaution the captain had everyone move to the higher levels and sealed all the airtight doors. A good deal of communicating equipment had been installed in the port engine room while the repairs were being made so there was a crystal clear view of what occurred next.

"They're punching through again at the same place," someone shouted. Though it wasn't the identical spot it was very close.

This time the hole was much smaller and whatever had made it withdrew instantly. There was only a single spurt of the frigid hydrogen-helium atmosphere that was cut off as something else came in through the opening, a thin brown tendril that projected a full yard into the room before it began to sag. When it touched the deck it ceased growing in length but the end began to swell as though the tendril were a tube that was inflating it. No one spoke as they watched the shape expand until it was the size and shape of a barrel covered with a shining and transparent coating. The top of the object writhed and shaped itself into a collection of nodules and there it stopped.

"What—what can it be?" Commander Rand asked, phrasing the question for all of them. The captain looked at it with fierce concentration.

"It's alien, it could be anything—but I'm hoping that it is a communicator of some sort." He switched on the phone in the engine room. "Hello—hello—can you hear me?"

A slit opened and gaped in the top of the barrel in the midst of the nodules and a pulsating, high-pitched sound bubbled out.

"Ha-rrr-rrr-ooo . . ." it screamed in vile imitation of a human voice. "Harrrooo . . ."

They worked with it during the coming weeks and learned to accept it. The men would have been rebellious and frightened if it weren't for the endless gravity that dragged at them and made life a continual torment. They were spending most of the time in the float beds where their bodies displaced the water so that the drag of gravity was relieved at least for a time. The captain and the ship's officers were taking turns teaching English to the biological communicator, which is what they thought the alien thing—they called it the barrel —to be. It seemed to have no intelligence of its own, yet it was alive underneath the hard coating that shielded it from the oxygen atmosphere. At first they read to it through a loud-speaker but when it showed no signs of either emotion or aggression they stayed in the compartment with it, near the door in case of emergency. The barrel would refuse to answer any questions—other than those directly involved with the language lessons—and after a few days they stopped trying. There had to be an eventual end to the instruction and they would find out what they wanted to know then. In the meantime the lessons were vitally important; they had to learn to communicate with the Jovians before they could find a way to convince them that they should remove the magnetic field that held them trapped.

In the middle of a lesson, at the end of the seventeenth day, the barrel suddenly stopped talking and withdrew the single eye that it had grown to look at the blackboard used for demonstrations. Rand, who was reading at the time, ran for the door and sealed it behind him. He watched from the control room with the others and when the eye opened again after a few minutes it had changed color and seemed to have a quality of intelligence about it that had been lacking before.

"What thing are you . . . ?" the barrel asked.

The conversation between the two differing life forms had begun.

Words and the simple mechanics of communication were easy enough for the Jovians to master, their memories appeared to be eidetic and no word was ever forgotten once explained. But referents were another thing. Nouns that could be pointed out, *chair, glass, knife,* were simple enough to convey, as well as easily demonstrable verbs, such as *walk, run* and *write.* When abstractions were reached communication of meaning became difficult and there were entire areas of misunderstanding.

"You come from where . . . ?" the Jovian asked, and when informed that they were from Earth, the third planet from the sun in this solar system, they asked "What is earths? What is planets? What is suns . . . ?"

Buried here, at the bottom of hundreds of miles of near-liquid atmosphere covered by solid layers of clouds, they had never seen the stars nor had they any inkling of knowledge that worlds other than their own existed. Yet they seemed to understand when it was explained to them, though they had very little interest and let the matter drop quickly and went on to something else. This was a pattern they seemed to follow—if they could be said to be following any pattern at all. They would pick a subject up, ask questions, then quickly abandon it. They (or it, the men in the ship never knew if they were talking to one or more Jovians) seemed to lack the simplest knowledge of the mechanical sciences, though they apparently absorbed explanations easily enough. There was only one thing that held their attention, that they kept coming back to: they never seemed satisfied with the answers.

"What thing are you . . . ?"

It was the captain who first understood something about them.

"The biological sciences," he said, "chemistry when it is biochemistry, neurophysics and all the rest. And electricity . . . of course! Bioelectricity."

"Sir . . . ?" Commander Rand asked.

"Those Jovians out there. Try to imagine the world they live in, from their point of view. They have no machines or artifacts that we have seen, yet they have intelligence and they have installed a device to communicate with us—even though they didn't recognize our own communicator. They must work with living matter alone and seem to have an incredible degree of control over it; look at the speed with which they constructed the barrel and installed it here."

"That's true, sir, and it explains a lot—but what about the magnetic field that is holding us down? They must have machines of some kind to generate that."

"Must they? Bioelectricity is well known on Earth, look at the electric eel. But let's ask them and find out. I think we have finally established a level of communication good enough to try that important question."

"There is a magnetic field at the base of this ship," he said, "do you know that?"

"Coming from electricity fields of force abide, yes . . ."
The barrel spoke clearly and precisely as ever, the single eye turning toward the captain, who stood at the far side of the engine room.

"Our ship cannot leave while that field exists, do you know that?"

"Yes . . ."

"Will you remove the field so that we may leave?"

"The fields of force will no longer rest . . . after the talking . . ."

It was a clear enough answer, except for the fact that they had a great deal of difficulty finding out exactly what *the talking* was. It obviously meant much more than conversation—but how much more? By indirection and suggestion the captain finally discovered that what they wanted to know about was human biology and that they wanted to examine living human cells.

"By *talking* they seem to mean *knowing about*. Gives some insight into how they think—though it doesn't help much."

He sent for a hypodermic needle and before the unblinking alien eye drew out some of his own blood. "Here . . ." the toneless voice said, and an opening gaped in the top of the barrel just below the eye. When Captain Bramley walked closer he could smell the sharp burn of ammonia: he emptied the hypodermic into the dark opening, which instantly rolled shut.

"There is talking we must do . . ." the voice spoke as the captain stepped away. "Talking to do of you . . ."

"I'll show you X-rays of human beings, there are also textbooks."

132

"There is talking to do with the eye . . ." The alien eye trembled a bit on top of its stalk as the captain stepped forward again.

"Don't get too close, sir," Rand called out. "We still can't be sure what they mean by the word talking."

"This time it appears to mean looking." The captain stopped. "After you have 'talked' to me with your eye will you release the ship?"

"The field of force will no longer rest after the talking . . ."

"I don't like it, captain!"

"Neither do I, but it sounds clear enough—or rather as clear as they ever get. Someone is going to have to be examined by the creature or we'll never leave. And I can't ask anyone else to volunteer for this."

The captain stepped forward again and the eye stretched forward as its stalk thinned and elongated. It hung quivering for a second before the captain's face before plunging forward into his chest and slashing down the length of his body, laying him open in one hideous wound that killed him instantly.

13

The Jovian stared out of the screen at the three earthmen, immobile and stolid. Yasumura gasped and unconsciously stepped backward a half step.

"What in Satan's name is that?" the general asked.

"Look for yourself," Sam said, pointing to the frost-covered wall. "Heavy supports, thick walls, a very cold pressure container big enough to half fill this compartment . . ."

"A Jovian!" Yasumura shouted. "They brought one back alive, and an ugly one at that. I didn't know there was any kind of life on Jupiter . . . ?"

"Obviously there is," Sam said. "But don't you have it reversed—about who did the bringing back? All the cables in the ship lead *here*—and this thing is still alive while every member of the expedition is dead . . ."

"Can it talk?" the general asked.

"Do the wire correct . . ." the Jovian's high-pitched and toneless voice sounded from the speaker. "The talking is impaired . . ."

"You're talking fine," Burke said. "Now you can tell us what you are doing here and how——" He broke off in midphrase and turned to Sam. "This is no accident! Do you think this creature has anything to do with the plague?"

"I think it is responsible for Rand's disease. I had something like this in mind when I asked you to come here. But would you have come if I suggested we would find *that?*"

"No, I would have thought you had cracked."

"So I couldn't explain to you. But you see—it had to be something like this. Everything about Rand's disease seems so *planned*, the timed mutations, the varying hosts, the incurability. If you look at it that way the disease stops being alien and instead is——"

"Artificial!"

"Right. And I think this creature here has had something to do with it. That's what I mean to find out now."

"Do the wire correct . . . the talking is impaired . . ." the Jovian said.

"The wire will be fixed after you have answered a few questions!" Sam realized that he was shouting; he lowered his voice. "Are you responsible for Rand's disease, for the sickness here in the city?"

"This is a meaningless . . ."

"A communication problem," Yasumura said. "This Jovian has learned English, undoubtedly from the men who manned this ship, but it has to relate the words to things in its own environment, which makes it impossible to get a one to one identity. Be very simple and clear when you ask a question, Sam—try and establish basics and build up from there."

Sam nodded. "I am a living creature, you are a living creature, do you understand me?"

"I am living . . ."

"When small living creatures live inside a larger creature and hurt it, it is called a disease. Do you understand?"

"What thing is hurt . . . ?"

"Hurt is not a thing, it is what happens—no, forget hurt for a moment. A disease is when a small creature breaks a big creature. Stops it. This is my arm—you see it—if I have

134

arm-disease from a small creature my arm falls off. If my arm falls off I am hurt. There are other ways small creatures can hurt my body. That is disease. Did you bring the disease that is hurting many people now?"

"I now know a disease is what . . . do the wire correct the talking is impaired . . ."

"The creature is being evasive, it won't tell us the truth," General Burke said.

Sam shook his head *no*. "We can't be sure of that. This last part sounded like it was offering a trade—fix the wires and it will talk. Can you hook up the ones I shot away? We can always cut them again."

"Take just a second," the engineer said. He touched the severed ends of the cables to each other lightly, then to the metal deck to see if they were carrying a heavy current. "No sparks so they shouldn't be lethal—I hope!" He quickly spliced the break in the wires.

"Did you bring the disease that is hurting my people?" Sam asked again. The Jovian pushed out an eye on a stalk to look at something to one side and not visible on the screen, then retracted it.

"Yes . . ." it said stolidly.

"But why?" Yasumura shouted. "Why did you do a dirty thing like this?"

"A talking has been done . . . what is a dirty thing?"

"Hold it awhile, Stanley, please," Sam asked as he pulled the engineer from before the screen. "I know why you're angry and I don't blame you, but it's no help now. This creature doesn't seem to have any emotions at all, so we're going to have to control ours." He turned back to the Jovian. "If you started this disease you must know how to stop it. Tell us how."

"The talking is not complete . . ."

"I don't know what you mean by *talking* and I don't care." The hatred of this creature that Sam had been containing broke through at last, he swung his gun up. "You saw what this gun can do, the way it tore up those wires, it can do the same thing to you, tear you up, tear up that tank you are in, tear you to pieces . . ."

"Stop it, Sam!" the general snapped, and pushed Sam's hand away from the trigger. The Jovian stared out at them, unmoved in any way that they could see. "You can't frighten that thing, you said yourself it has no emotions the way we know them, maybe it isn't even afraid of dying. There has to be another way to get to it——"

"There is," Sam said, pulling himself from the general's grasp. "We have already found out one thing it doesn't like —having those wires cut—so maybe we should cut a few more."

The general jumped forward, but Sam was faster. He spun on his heel and the gun hammered out a torrent of slugs that howled away, ricocheting and tearing holes in the walls, chewing their way through the massed cables: electricity arced and spat and the shots boomed deafeningly in the enclosed space. Burke tore the gun from him just as he let up on the trigger.

"That stirred the beast up!" Yasumura pointed to the screen. The Jovian was writhing, turning back and forth while its eyestalks swung about jerkily.

"The talking is not complete . . . the many wires are not complete . . ."

"The many wires and the damned talking and everything are going to stay not complete until you give us what we want!" Sam leaned forward until his face almost touched the screen. "Give us what we need to stop your disease."

"The talking is not complete . . ."

"Sam, let me fix the wires, you may kill the thing . . ."

"No I won't—it doesn't look uncomfortable, just unhappy. All the wires we traced came from the radio and television pickups; they are feeding the Jovian information of some kind, that must be what it means by the talking. And the talking is not going to be complete until it helps us. Do you hear that?" he shouted into the screen. "The talking is not complete. Give me what I want then I will fix the wires. Give it now."

The Jovian stopped moving and the eyestalks withdrew until the head was just wrinkled slits again. "You shall . . . must shall . . . complete the wires . . ."

"*After* I get it."

"Complete . . ."

"*After!*"

His shout echoed away down the metal compartment and was followed by silence. They stared at each other, man and alien, or more correctly alien and alien—for this is what they were to each other. Alien, meaning different, alien meaning unknown. They faced each other in silent communication for the choice had been clearly stated by both of them and there was nothing more to be said until one or the other of them decided to act.

"Sam . . ." Yasumura started forward, but General Burke's fingers clamped onto his arm and whipped him back.

"Let him be," the general muttered. "He's laid it out clear and simple and I'm glad he did it because I don't know if I would have had the guts to."

"*After!*" Sam shouted into the silence and raised his gun again toward the cables, over half of which had been cut by the last burst.

The Jovian slid sideways and vanished from the screen.

"What is it up to?" Yasumura asked as he rubbed away some of the sweat that was dripping into his eyes.

"I don't know," Sam said grimly, "but I'm going to hurry it up."

He held his hand out to the general who reluctantly passed back the gun. Sam fired a short burst that cut two more of the electric cables. An instant later there was a booming that jarred the wall above the phone screen.

"Get back!" Burke shouted and hit Yasumura with his shoulder, knocking him aside.

With a rending screech something came through the solid metal of the wall and crashed to the deck. A screaming of released pressure tore at their ears and from the hole came a jet of frigid gas that filled the space around them with clouds of burning vapor. As they drew back the roaring jet cut off and the vapor swirled and dissipated. They looked down at the foot-long, gray cylinder that had cracked open when it hit the metal flooring, disclosing another cylinder inside made of some mottled and purple substance. This was rotting and falling away as they watched, giving off an intense odor of ammonia that drove them away from it. There was a lemon-yellow layer inside this, then still another—all of them melting and dropping to pieces under the corrosive attack of the earth's air.

This seething process lasted for almost three minutes and at some moment during this time the Jovian reappeared on the screen but no one noticed it. When the pool of liquid on the floor ceased bubbling there remained only a waxy, translucent cylinder the size of a six-inch length of broomstick. Sam used his gun barrel to roll it from the puddle and bent over to examine it more closely. When it moved he saw that it was hollow with quite thin walls and seemed to be filled with a liquid.

"The talking is will be complete . . . do the wires correct . . ."

14

"Is it . . . a cure for the plague?" General Burke asked, staring down at the capsule of liquid. "It could be a trick of some kind——"

"The wires correct . . ." the flat voice squealed from the speaker.

"I'll get into that," Yasumura said, taking out his knife. "What a mess—it's a good thing that they're color coded."

Sam took off his beret and picked up the waxy tube with it. "I hope it's the cure—but we won't know until we've tried." He looked down at it, startled. "It's not cold! Yet it should be frozen solid at the temperature inside that tank. This may be it, Cleaver!"

"Then let's get it out where it can do some good. I want a phone and I want to know where the elevator is—in that order."

"Yes, sir, General," the engineer said, twisting together the ends of a severed wire and reaching for another one. "You'll find them both down there. Follow the bulkhead that way and out the first door; they're in the corridor outside. Send someone back to let me know what happens. I'll stick here and wire up this heavyweight Jovian, then see if I can get him to talk some more."

General Burke called the phone that was located on the deck nearest to the air lock and after tapping his fingers for an impatient thirty seconds the screen cleared as Lieutenant Haber answered. "Report," the general snapped.

"Quiet now, sir. The firing stopped some time ago but they have the lights on and the opening ranged and they must have a scope on it. I tried to take a look awhile ago and they almost blew my head off. So far they haven't tried to get in."

"Hold there, Haber, and keep under cover. I'll contact them so we can get out of this ship. It looks as if we may have a cure for the plague but we're going to have to get to a hospital to prove it." He rang off before the startled officer could answer. "I'm going up to the control room, Sam. Tell Yasumura that he is to join Haber at the lock as soon as he has finished the wiring job and make him understand that it is important. Then join me in control."

By the time Sam had delivered the message—and convinced the engineer that now was not the time to talk to the Jovian—General Burke had found the way back to the control room and was shouting into the radiophone. He had cleaned most of the blackout cream from his face so there would be no doubt of his identity. When Sam came in he waved him toward the phone.

"You know Chabel of World Health, you talk to him. He doesn't believe a word I say." Professor Chabel stared out of the screen at them, white-faced and trembling.

"How can I believe what you say, General Burke, or whatever Dr. Bertolli tells me, after what has happened? The Emergency Council is in session right now and do you know what they're considering——? I don't dare say it on an open circuit . . ."

"I know what they're considering," Sam said, in as controlled a voice as possible. "They want to start dropping H-bombs and atomize Zone-Red—New York City and all the area within a hundred miles of it. But they don't have to do this, there is a chance now that we can stop Rand's disease." He held up the capsule. "I think this contains the cure and there is only one way to find out, get it to Bellevue as soon as we can."

"No!" Chabel said, his voice quavering. "If you do not leave the ship there is a chance that the Emergency Council will not take any desperate measures. You will stay where you are."

"I would like to talk to Dr. McKay, I can explain to him what we have found."

"Impossible. Dr McKay is still ill after his heart attack, in any case I would not allow you to speak to him . . ." Sam reached out and broke the circuit, then signaled for the operator to put in a call to Dr. McKay.

"Damned old woman," the general said angrily. "Hysterical. Does he think that *I* am lying?"

The call signal chimed but it was Eddie Perkins, not McKay, who appeared on the screen.

"*You!*" he said, taut with anger. "Haven't you caused enough trouble? I heard what you have done at the airport, you must be insane——"

"Eddie!" Sam broke in, "shut up. I'm not going to feud with you any more. This is the only chance you are going to have in your entire life to make up for some of the mistakes you made. Help me now and the matter will end there. I must talk to Dr. McKay, General Burke here will tell you why. General Burke of the United Nations Army—you recognize him—and you can believe him."

"It is very simple, Dr. Perkins. We are in the 'Pericles' now and we have discovered the cause of Rand's disease. Dr. Bertolli here has the serum that will cure it. We must leave this ship and go to Bellevue Hospital at once. We are being stopped from doing this and Dr. McKay is the only man who can help us. Now, if you will connect us . . ."

He said it in a matter-of-fact way, simplifying the situation and using the crisp tones of command that admitted no other choice. Sam looked at Eddie Perkins, who sat silently chewing his lip in agony, and realized for the first time that Perkins was without malice, he was just in a situation that was too big for him, that he was unequipped to handle and was too afraid to admit that he had been doing badly.

"Put us through, Eddie," Sam said softly.

"McKay is a sick man."

"He'll be dead like the rest of us soon if Rand's disease isn't stopped. Put the call through, Eddie . . ."

Perkins made a convulsive movement toward the switch and his image faded from the screen. They waited tensely, not looking at each other, while the hold signal swirled its endless circles. When McKay's face finally appeared on the screen Sam let out his breath: he had not realized that he had been holding it.

"What is it, Sam?" McKay asked, sitting up in a hospital bed, looking strained and gaunt but still alert. He listened intently while Sam explained what they had found in the ship and what had been done, nodding in agreement.

"I believe it, simply because I never believed in Rand's disease. It has acted in an impossible manner from the first. Now this is completely understandable if it was a manufactured and designed disease. But why—no, never mind that for now. What is it you want me to do?"

"We want to get this liquid to the team at Bellevue at once, but we're trapped in this ship. Professor Chabel's orders."

"Nonsense! I can talk to one or two people and do something about those orders. I was placed in command of the team to discover a treatment for Rand's disease, and if you have one there I want it *now*." He rang off.

"Game old boy," the general said. "I hope his heart lasts until he gets some action out of those mumble-brained politicians. Come on, Sam, let's get down to the air lock and see if those chuckleheads will let us out."

Lieutenant Haber and Stanley Yasumura were resting against the corridor wall, well away from the line of fire through the partially opened door.

"Stay where you are," General Burke said as Haber started to struggle up. "Anything to report?"

"Negative, sir, unchanged since I talked to you last."

"We want to open that outer door again since we should be getting out of here soon. Is that junction box in the line of fire?"

"I don't think so, sir. Not if you were to stay flat on the floor until you got to it, but I think if you stood up you could be seen from outside."

"Tell me what has to be done, will you, Stanley," Sam said. "I'll take care of it."

"I would love to," the engineer said, biting his teeth together hard to control their growing tendency to chatter, "but it would take too long and you would take too long doing it and—I'm the one who has to do it so let me get going before my nerve fails completely. Just pay this wire out to me as I go. And wish me luck."

He dropped flat at the open inner door, hesitated just a moment, then crawled through the opening. Nothing happened as he made his way around the wall to the open junction box, nor did he draw any attention even when he had to stand up to connect the wires. But on the return journey he must have been seen because bullets drummed on the outer door and the hull and some found the tiny opening and ricocheted around the air lock. Yasumura dived through into the hall and lay there exhausted but unharmed.

"Good work," the general said. "Now let's open the outer door and see how those gun-happy police react."

As soon as he was able to stand, the engineer made the connections to the power pack and closed the circuit. The circuit breakers had cooled off and automatically reset themselves: the motor whined and the outer door began to open slowly.

A hail of bullets was the first reaction, but they were well out of the line of fire.

"Shaky trigger fingers," the general said contemptuously. "I wonder if they have any idea of what they hope to accomplish by this."

Others must have shared his opinion because the fire broke off suddenly and was replaced by an echoing silence. Almost fifteen minutes passed before someone shouted from outside.

"General Burke, can you hear me?"

"I can hear you all right," Burke bellowed back, "but I can't see you. Are those nervous policemen going to shoot me if I enter the air lock?"

"No, sir . . . we have orders not to."

If the general was concerned he did not show it. He straightened his beret, flicked some of the dried mud from his coveralls and strode forward to the rim of the air lock, standing straight and unmoving in the glare from the lights that flooded in.

"Now what is it?" he called down. "And turn those lights down—are you trying to blind me?" There were some muffled commands and two of the lights went out.

"We have received orders that you are to be allowed to leave the ship." The speaker came forward, a grizzled police captain.

"I'll want transportation. A copter."

"We have one here——"

"Warm it up. And what happened to my sergeant?"

"If you mean the one who was firing at us, he's dead."

The general turned around without another word and stamped inside. "Let's go before they change their minds." He had the fixed, unhappy look that soldiers get who have seen too many friends die.

"You won't need me any more," Yasumura said. "So if you don't mind I'll stay here and take a look at the ship's log and have some chitchat with that overweight passenger."

"Yes, of course," the general said. "Thank you for the aid . . ."

"Wrong way around, General, I'm the one who should be thanking you for getting me back into the ship."

A service lift truck was backed up to the "Pericles" and its platform raised to the level of the air lock. They stepped out onto it, carrying the wounded lieutenant between them, and the operator swung it around in an arc and dropped it to ground level; a few yards away was a copter with its blades slowly turning. They ignored the grim-faced and heavily armed policemen who stood around watching them. Sam held the capsule tightly in his free hand as they helped Haber into the copter and laid him down gently across the rear row of seats.

"Bellevue Hospital, just as fast as you can make it." Sam dropped down next to the police pilot. The man said nothing but opened his throttle and the machine leaped into the air.

Ahead of them the light-dotted skyline of Manhattan grew larger and before it, just as real as the buildings for Sam, swam the memory of Nita's face, swollen and ill. It had been hours since he had last seen her and he knew she would be worse now, far worse—or perhaps . . . he would not accept the thought. She couldn't be dead, not now with salvation so close. Or was it? He looked down at the waxy cylinder in his lap; it was soft and it gave when he squeezed it. Could it really contain a cure? Memory of the past hours reassured him. It had to be right. What would the Jovian have gained by giving them the wrong substance? Or why should it bother to give them the right one? Both questions were meaningless since he had no idea what motivated the alien. The copter swung around the bulk of the hospital, locked onto the control beam and was brought in for a landing. Two attendants hurried toward them.

"Take care of the patient in here," Sam called as he jumped down from the door and pushed by them, knocking one aside when he didn't move fast enough. Before Sam reached the entrance he was running and at the elevator he pounded his free hand against the wall until the doors opened. General Burke jumped in after him.

"Easy, boy," he said, "you'll get there soon enough."

It was dark in the room and he turned on all the ceiling lights. There was a moan from the bed where a strange woman shielded her eyes from the sudden glare: he wheeled to the other bed. My God, how bad she looked. Nita . . .

"What are you doing here? Who are you? Get out at once!" A doctor he had never seen before was pulling at his

143

arm and he realized how he must look with his mud-stained coveralls and blackened skin.

"I'm sorry, Doctor, but I'm Dr. Bertolli. If you have a hypodermic——" He broke off as he saw the autoclave against the far wall and hurried over to it, kicking the floor switch to open the lid.

The contents were still hot and he burned his fingers as he assembled a hypodermic needle, but he didn't notice this, nor was he aware of the general, who had drawn the doctor aside and was explaining in a low voice.

The capsule. He swabbed the end with alcohol and pushed the needle against it: it slid through easily. Was this a treatment for Rand's—or was it poison? How could he know? He inverted the capsule and drew back the plunger on the needle until the barrel was half full of straw-colored liquid. He pulled out the needle and handed the capsule to General Burke, who had appeared at his shoulder.

"Keep that end up," he said as he gently took Nita's arm from under the covers and, working with one hand, swabbed alcohol on the inside of her elbow. Her skin was dry, burning hot, lumped here and there with the swollen red nodules. Nita! He forced his mind away from her as a person, she was a patient, his patient. He massaged her vein with his thumb until it expanded, then slid the needle into it. How much? Five cc's for a start, then more if it was needed.

On the telltale her temperature read one hundred and six degrees and in conjunction with the recordings of her blood pressure and pulse showed that she was dying. Her deep rasping breathing broke off suddenly and her back arched under the covers: she gave a deep chattering moan. He reached out and touched her in panic—what had he done? Had he killed her?

But when he looked back at the telltale he saw that her temperature had dropped to one hundred and five.

It was unnatural the way it happened, and completely impossible. Yet so was Rand's disease. As they watched, in a matter of a few minutes, the disease was destroyed. Within five minutes her temperature was normal and within fifteen the flushed swellings had changed color and begun to subside. Her breathing steadied, became smooth and deep.

When she opened her eyes she looked up at them and smiled.

"Sam, darling . . . whatever are you doing with your face painted up like that?"

144

15

"Dr. McKay sent me," Eddie Perkins said when Sam turned around. He was surprised to find that there were at least a dozen people in the room with him.

"Here," Sam said, handing him the hypodermic needle. "Take this and the capsule the general is holding—keep it upright—and get them to the team at once. Tell them this is the cure for Rand's disease. Be careful with it, I don't know what it is and there is no more where it came from, at least not right now. Microanalysis—they'll know what to do. I'll call Dr. McKay and tell him what has happened."

"He's under sedation, you'll have to wait until the morning. We were afraid of the strain he . . . he was quite forceful in arranging that you be let out of the ship." Perkins started away cradling the hypo and the capsule in his cupped hands, but he halted for an instant at the door and turned. "Listen, Sam . . . thanks . . ." He hurried out.

Nita was sound asleep and Sam was washing the dye from his hands and face when the general reappeared.

"You have five minutes," he said. "I've had a call from Dr. Yasumura at the ship and he wants us out there right away. I've had enough of the police for one day, thank you, so I sent for my own transportation and it's on the way up here from the fort now. Is this going to work, Sam?"

"I don't know," he answered, toweling himself dry. "The Jovian gave us the cure all right—you saw how it worked with Nita—but there's not enough in that capsule to treat fifty people, and there must be fifty thousand cases by now. It's all up to the team in the lab. If they can analyze it, break it down and build it up again on their own then the plague is over. I certainly hope they can."

"What are the odds?"

"No odds at all—or a billion to one. All we can do is wait and see. And go back to the 'Pericles' and try and

145

make some sense out of the Jovian conversation. Did Stanley say what he wanted?"

"I didn't talk to him. Just got the message to come at once."

When they came out on the copter platform Sam was surprised to see that it was already light, the last stars were fading in the west and the sky had that clean-washed look that you only see after a rain. A rumble of heavy engines sounded from the south and grew to a roar as a flight of five heavy VTO craft thundered overhead. They began to circle as one of them dropped straight down toward the hospital below, aiming for the platform where the two men waited.

"When you said transportation I thought you meant a copter," Sam shouted above the roar of the propellers. "Those vertical-take-off things aren't even supposed to land here."

"I know all that, but being a general has its compensations. And I'm still not in love with those police at the airport so I thought a little waving of the big stick might quiet them down . . ."

His words were drowned in the howl of the engine as the plane touched the platform lightly, then settled down onto its landing gear. The blast of sound died to a mutter as the canopy slid open and the pilot leaned out. "They told me you wanted this, sir," he said, passing down the belt and holster with the long-barreled, chrome, teak-handled pistol in it.

"Now that's more comfortable," General Burke said, settling it into place on his thigh before he climbed up into the plane.

Sam followed him. It was a tight squeeze with the three of them in the cockpit, and as soon as the canopy was shut the plane hurled itself into the air. The other VTO planes closed in around it while it was still rising and they all swung over into horizontal flight in a practiced maneuver and headed eastward toward Kennedy Airport. They came in high and first swung in a rapid circle above the towering projectile of the "Pericles" before settling down slowly next to it. The blunt nose slid by and the length of the scarred gray hull as they grounded together near the base. This time the stares of the police were not as menacing as they walked through the gap that had been opened in the barbed wire, to the landing ramp pushed up below the open air lock.

"Has anyone entered this ship?" the general snapped at the two policemen who were on guard at the base.

"No, sir—we've had orders that——"

"That's fine. No one is to enter."

He pushed by before he had a chance to hear what the orders were and stamped up the metal steps: Sam followed him through the air lock and into the elevator. Stanley Yasumura was slumped down in the captain's chair on the bridge and waved them over when they entered.

"It's all on the record," he said. "The log was kept right up to the very end; the men who manned this ship had guts, but really."

"What do you mean?" Sam asked.

"The 'Pericles' was trapped right after they landed, something to do with a magnetic field that the Jovians' generated. I skipped over the early part fast but you can go back and hear it for yourself. Then the natives contacted the crew, learned English and killed the captain—just like that, opened him up and called it *talking.*"

"That's the same word the Jovian here used—what do they mean by it?"

"I would like to find out the answer to that one myself— I've been trying to get through to our specimen, but he won't answer his phone. Anyway, the men on Jupiter thought that it meant total understanding or total comprehension, or maybe the understanding of basic life processes. The Jovians apparently have no machines and never developed a machine culture—but what they do have is a bioculture. They seem to be able to do whatever they want with living cells. They acted like kids with a new toy when the ship landed with a different life form; they wanted to take them apart to see what made them tick. And they did, one by one, tracked down the crewmen and dissected them . . ."

"Hell is cold, just as Dante wrote," General Burke said as he softly stroked the butt of his pistol. "They're devils right out of the Old Testament, no souls, no feelings. We're just going to have to outfit this ship again and go back there with a hold full of H-bombs . . ."

"No, Cleaver, you have it wrong," Sam said. "They're a different life form and they obviously think and feel—if they can feel—differently from us. They didn't ask the crew of the 'Pericles' if they wanted to be taken to pieces to be examined, but do we ask laboratory. rats if they want to be dissected or do we give the chickens any choice between growing up or being given vile diseases while they are still in the eggs?"

"Nonsense! We can't ask questions of rats and eggs, nor do we want to . . ."

"You're right. So maybe the Jovians can't ask us the right questions—or maybe they just don't want to. Perhaps they take each other apart the same way without asking permission, so why should they ask us?"

"That's what some of them thought on the 'Pericles,'" Yasumura said. "The first officer, Weeke, he always talked like a stolid Dutchman but he had a real imagination, theoretical physics. He put his theory into the log that the Jovian individuals weren't really. individual but had a single mass mind. If this is true, they wouldn't care in the slightest if they were killed, as individuals, any more than a fingernail cares when it gets clipped off. And if that's the only. kind of existence they knew, they would automatically assume that we are the same—so they would have started taking us apart with great pleasure."

"It's only a theory," General Burke rumbled.

"But it explains a lot. Either every Jovian is a sizzing genius or there is one mind big enough to handle almost everything. It—or they—learned to speak English just as fast as it could be read to them. And they had never even seen or imagined there could be machines, yet they mastered machine technology in a matter of days, almost contemptuously. They needed to use it to work inside the alien environment of the ship, to build that pressure tank down below and control the ship, so they learned what they had to."

"Wasn't there any resistance to all this?"

"A good. deal, but all ineffective." Yasumura turned on the log and began scanning for the entry he wanted. "Maybe in the beginning before the Jovians were established in the ship something might have been done, though it is hard to imagine what. Remember, they couldn't take off.and short of blowing up the ship and themselves with it there was little they could really do. Anyway, here's how it ended; this is the last entry in the log made by Commander Rand." He pressed the playback button.

". . . May twenty-fourth according to the bridge clock, but we're not keeping track of the time any more. I shouldn't say we—they got Anderson a little while ago and he was the last one, I mean outside of me. Those tendril things can go through any kind of metal and they are all through the ship now and there's no way to cut them. One touch and you're paralyzed and that's the end of that. I saw what they did to him too. He's down on C deck in one of those tanks right next to two of the others. All of them keep getting sick, then getting cured, though they don't look the same afterward and finally they die. I've never seen anything like . . . they must have mutated the diseases from germs they found in our bodies or I don't know what . . ."

There was a rattling noise, then a crash of glass before Rand began speaking again, and his voice was thicker. "If I sound like I have been drinking, I have, because it's a little hard to bear, you know, with everyone else . . ." He stopped, and when he continued he sounded much better. "But I've broken the bottle because I can't be drunk to do what I have to do. Listen, whoever you are, I hope you never hear this. I hope I can get through to the engine room and do what I have to do. I'm going to knock out all the safeties and crank up the pile until it blows. That's just my suicide because the rest are dead or should be dead. Those things out there are smart and they're going to learn all about us and learn how to fly this ship and then I don't know what they're planning to do. But I want to stop them. This is Commander Rand, closing the log, the day is May twenty-fourth and one way or another there are going to be no more entries in this log." The loud-speaker rustled with background noise but there was nothing else after this.

Yasumura reached out and flicked it off and it was a while before anyone said anything.

"He was right," General Burke said. "They did bring their hellish disease and try to destroy us all."

"No, they didn't," Sam said. "What they did here looks more like a laboratory experiment than any deliberate attempt to wipe us out. The way they tailor-made a disease to fit earthly conditions, to attack animals they had never seen, to mutate under these conditions, means they have a perfect or almost perfect knowledge and control of biochemistry at every level. We still have no idea of how they spread the virus from the ship, sending it across Long Island in almost a straight line—a physical impossibility by our state of knowledge. If they had wanted to they could have released a plague that would have spread around the world and have wiped us out in a day. But they didn't."

"Then what *were* they trying to accomplish . . . ?" the general started to say, but Stanley Yasumura cut him off.

"Look at those needles jump—there's juice being fed into the high-power rig, the ultrafrequency radio!" The radiophone buzzed and he turned to answer it: a uniformed man appeared on the screen.

"This is the tower, what are you broadcasting? We're getting interference on our navigating frequencies . . ."

"Not us, but there is a thing in a tank downstairs that has cut into all the circuits. What does the signal sound like?"

"Just a moment, I'll hook it into this circuit. And see if you can't do something about cutting it off; it has harmonics that are lousing up almost all of our operating frequencies."

The voice died and a moment later was replaced by a high-pitched, shrieking moan that set their nerves on edge like a fingernail on glass. The engineer quickly cut the volume down to a sinister mutter.

"What on earth is that?" General Burke asked.

"Better say 'what on Jupiter.' In a strange way it sounds something like the Jovian's voice. Stanley, could that signal get through to Jupiter and be understood there?"

"I don't see why not—if there is a good receiver out there, that frequency should cut right through the Heaviside layer and be detectable that far out if it has enough power behind it. But, do you mean . . . ?"

"I don't mean anything, I'm just wondering—— Look, those meters just dropped back to zero. What's happening?"

Yasumura checked them, then other instruments in the room. "No power being drawn at all any more. Wonder what our friend in the tank is up to?"

"Let's get down there," Sam said, starting for the door.

The first thing they noticed when they emerged from the elevator was the sharp smell of ammonia that the blowers were laboring to remove from the air; they started to run. The deck near the reinforced wall of the pressure tank was running with moisture as was the wall of the tank itself. The layer of frost had vanished.

"The tank has warmed up . . . !"

"And the pressurized atmosphere is gone from it too, I imagine," Sam said, looking at the darkened phone screen.

"Then the thing is dead—it committed suicide," the general said. "But why——?"

Sam shook his head. "I wonder if we really can call it suicide? That Jovian in there probably never had any intention or desire to return to its own planet. It came here to do a job —or maybe to make an experiment, that might be a better description. Our world was its laboratory and we were the experimental animals. The experiment was finished, it made its report——"

"The radio signal!"

"—when everything was gone. So it died, or disconnected, or whatever you want to call it. Function performed. About as unemotional as an epithelial cell in your skin; it protects your body, dies and falls off."

"One consolation," General Burke kicked out at the tangle of cables. "At least it had to report its mission or its experiment a failure."

"Did it?" Sam asked. "Perhaps it was a social experiment, not a medical one. They certainly knew beforehand how the disease would affect our bodies, so perhaps it was our social grouping or our science they were interested in. How we would combat the disease, what we would do when we found they had caused it. After all, they made no real attempt to hide the fact they had brought it—the log is still here and once the door was opened the Jovian's presence was obvious. And it had the capsule ready, don't forget that. Once it understood the threat to cut off all communication it delivered the thing at once . . ."

There was the sound of running footsteps and they turned to see Eddie Perkins in the doorway.

"I tried to call you on the radiophone but I couldn't get through," he said, gasping a bit as he caught his breath.

"What is it?"

"Rand's . . . Rand's disease. The cure. We can duplicate the stuff in the capsule. It's all over. We have it licked."

16

A gust of wind hurled a spattering of snowflakes against the outside of the window, where they hung for long seconds until the heat of the room melted them and they ran down the pane. Killer Dominguez, sitting reversed on the chair with his arms leaning on the back, blew a jet of cigarette smoke toward the window.

"Turning into a real crummy day, just look at that. If I didn't have arthritis already I would catch it today. Sorry to see you go, Doc."

"I'm not sorry to leave, Killer," Sam said, digging a handful of white socks out of the dresser drawer and dumping them into the suitcase that lay open on the bed. "This is a great room for an intern to live in, it's handy to the work and bearable because you don't see it much. But it's a little too spartan—reminds me too much of the Army."

"And also no place for a married man, right, Doc?"

"There's that too," Sam smiled. "I can just see myself carrying Nita over this threshold. About the only thing I'm sorry about leaving is the ambulance. I'll miss your driving, Killer."

"No, you won't, Doc. It'll be easier on your heart once you're off the meat wagon. They'll need you in this new Lab 30 program, what with you knowing all about the Jovians and such. I hear that they got the idea from them."

"In a way." He closed the dresser and went to the closet. "It was the cure for Rand's disease that the Jovians gave to us that started the entire thing off; it's an entirely new concept in medicine. The J-molecule, that's what they're calling it, appears to be alive like a virus or a microorganism and capable of reproducing itself easily. That's how they managed to make enough of it so fast to stop Rand's disease in a matter of days. You just put it on a petri dish and fission begins."

"Great—instant medicine! That will put the drugstores out of business—everyone grows their own."

"It might at that. We're just beginning to find out what the J-molecule can do and if it turns out to be just one-tenth as effective as it seems to be we should thank the Jovians for bringing us the plague—and the cure—because it is going to make such a basic change in medicine."

"C'mon, Doc—think of how many were killed . . ."

"I'm thinking of how many are going to live, because thousands and eventually millions of lives will be saved for every one that died. You see not only does the J-molecule reproduce itself but under certain conditions it can be trained to attack other diseases. Then the new strain is specific only for the disease it has been trained to attack—and it breeds true."

"Now you're getting outta my depth, Doc. I bring 'em in, you patch 'em up, let's leave it at that. What's the big hush-hush rumor I hear about another ship to Jupiter? Not enough trouble from the first time?"

"Is there anything you don't hear, Killer?"

"I got my contacts."

Sam closed the bag and locked it. "So far we're only a pressure group that are trying to convince the UN that the Jovians aren't really inimical, but we're having heavy going. They're still too much afraid. But we'll have to go back there someday and contact them and this time we want it to be a friendly contact. All volunteers, I imagine, and safeguards will have to be worked out to make sure nothing like Rand's disease reoccurs."

Nita had opened the door while he was talking but his back was toward her and he hadn't noticed.

"And I suppose you would like to volunteer?" she asked, brushing drops of melted snow from her coat.

He kissed her first, well and long. Killer nodded approval and ground out his cigarette. "I gotta be moving, duty calls." He waved good-by as he left.

"Well, you didn't answer me," she said.

He held her at arm's length, suddenly serious.

"You wouldn't stop me, would you?"

"I wouldn't like it, darling, but no—I wouldn't stop you, how could I? But please, not for a while . . ."

"Not for a good long while, and in any case I wouldn't be going alone. Stan Yasumura is in on the project and Haber will be with us as soon as he can get off crutches—even Cleaver Burke is on our side. I don't know how he wangled it, but he managed to get assigned to the Space Commission—he's even going to space-fitness school so he can be with the second expedition."

"The poor man, at his age! All those free-fall exercises and multiple-G stress chambers. I feel sorry for him."

"I don't," Sam said, and taking her by the arm, picking up the suitcase in his other hand, he started for the door. "I feel sorrier for the Jovians."